WARNING! THE CONTENT OF THIS
BOOK CAN CAUSE OUTBURST OF
UNCONTROLLABLE LAUGHTER.

(CONTAINS GRAPHIC ADULT LANGUAGE)

GENERATION X : URBAN REALITY

TEEN EXPLOITS & COMEDIC SITUATIONS

DAVE WILLIAMS (MAED)

authorHOUSE®

AuthorHouse™
1663 Liberty Drive
Bloomington, IN 47403
www.authorhouse.com
Phone: 833-262-8899

Published by AuthorHouse 01/19/2021

ISBN: 978-1-6655-1398-2 (sc)
ISBN: 978-1-6655-1399-9 (hc)
ISBN: 978-1-6655-1407-1 (e)

Library of Congress Control Number: 2021900963

Print information available on the last page.

This book aims to entertain book lovers that enjoy reading unique, creative works of realistic fiction.

CONTENTS

CHAPTER ONE

THE 911 CALL

When a group of complex personalities is mandated under the same roof for an extended period, situations in everyday life can change drastically. As a result, strange, outlandish behavioral conditioning can lead to situations of mischief, mayhem, and chaos. Character differences can range from the wild and reckless to the absurd and sometimes ridiculous.

During the early 1990s, the recession caused an economic decline, which created a drastic change in workforce stability. It challenged the lives and the day-to-day existence of people across the country. Fortunately, two girls whose mother had a bit of luck during these hard- times; her job wasn't shutting down or relocating to Mexico or somewhere overseas. Instead, it moved to a more established, industrial city about sixty miles away from their original home.

Anyway, this news was good to hear. Still, Tamara and her younger sister, Earlene, had to move in with their Grandmother across town. Furthermore, they had to endure the antics from an irritating, pain-in-the-ass cousin of theirs—Alvin Junior—aka A. J. He had moved there with his dad and sister months earlier. Nevertheless, A. J. was their main concern, and they couldn't dismiss their feeling of dread from being in a situation like this.

It was the first day of summer, and Earlene was already sick of A. J. He was a pest, a clown, and a want-ta-be comedian. He told dumb jokes, and he thought he was the hottest sensation since Eddie Murphy. To his friends, he was a laugh-a-minute and fun to be around—whatever he said or did to get a laugh seemed to amuse them. But when it came to Earlene and Tamara, he fell short; he was about as funny as a train wreck.

Underneath A. J.'s facade of playfulness and joking, he had a ton of love for Tamara and Earlene. But all he ever managed to do was get on their very last nerve. Furthermore, the way A. J. kept pushing Earlene's stress button was an ongoing ritual, as common as the wind blowing.

For example, there was an event that brought sparks to Earlene's growing disdain for A. J. It happened on a Saturday morning in June. A bicycle wreck occurred that morning, which could be best described more like a tragedy. Earlene's knowledge of the incident came from an anonymous phone call. Someone saw what happened and called her about it before A.J. even knew that she knew. And it was painfully obvious that hearing the news would make her blood boil. So when she found out that it was A.J. who wrecked her ten-speed bicycle, her instinct to kick his ass kicked in.

The story was that Mr. No-hands-No-feet-No-two front teeth, A.J.- the-Great took Earlene's bicycle out for a spin through the neighborhood without her permission. The ridiculous part about it was that common sense didn't tell the genius that riding a bike thirty-five miles per hour down a steep hill, trying to make a forty-five degree turn around a corner without using the breaks would wind up with him hitting the ground.

And that's just how it happened. A.J. hit the ground and rolled like a log off the back of a lumber truck—right into a fire hydrant on the corner. And while he was rolling, Earlene's bike slid underneath the rolling wheels of a garbage truck. After the bike was pulled from beneath the truck, it was shaped like a pretzel, and it looked like a pile of abstract art. But, even more heart-wrenching was when old funky Herald-the-trash man picked it up without thinking twice about how it got there and threw it in the back of the truck with the rest of the trash.

Meanwhile, after the strenuous contemplation of a lie to tell Earlene, A.J. went home and tried to sneak through the back door. He had a blood-soaked paper towel covering his mouth because his two front teeth were missing. He even had scrapes and scratches on the side of his face and arms, but before he could say a word to Earlene, she saw the little creep and didn't have any sympathy for him at all. As far as she was concerned, what he did was wrong, and he was going to pay!

So, like a flash of lightning, she jumped on his ass like a thunderstorm. She grabbed him by his throat and tried to choke the life out of him. His eyes popped out of his head, and blood trickled from the side of his mouth and ran down his chin. But fortunately, and right on time, Grandma came from the back room and stopped her, just as she was drawing back her fist to coldcock him into the middle of next summer. Grandma snatched her by the collar, took her off him, and sat her down in a chair. But by the time she turned back around to scold A.J., he was gone. He had escaped from this situation like a fugitive on a chain gang.

This was a close call for A.J. Even though his dad, Alvin senior, and Grandma Ella did their best to calm Earlene down and didn't have to use a straitjacket, they both knew that Earlene had a temper just like her mother, Erma Jean. Pushing the wrong button on either one of them was like pushing the button on a time bomb for terror.

Meanwhile, A.J.'s sister, Danielle, was trying to show her concern for Earlene as well. And, to show that her heart was in the right place, and to save her weasel of a brother's life, she made a cold pitcher of cherry Kool-Aid and brought her a cup to cool her off. But in all practicality, she was hoping it might quench her thirst for the taste of blood.

Uncle Alvin reassured her that he would buy her a new bicycle and punish A. J. when he caught up with him. Her Grandma promised to talk with A. J. about her bike, and the many other things he did to aggravate her.

In short, Earlene knew that their intentions were good and that they both meant well. But she also knew A. J. and she knew that getting through to him was like peeling back the layers of a rotten onion. To put it plain and simple, the idea of revenge was still firmly planted in the back of her mind. She just knew that when she caught up with that little rat again—he was going to be an astronaut—and she had the rocket-ship to fly his ass to the moon.

Three days later, A. J. surfaced. Everyone knew he was hiding somewhere in the attic, but as long as he stayed out of their sight, he couldn't cause any more trouble. The anger and resentment that Earlene had been feeling subsided to a smaller degree, which is just what A.J. hoped would happen. But he was still acting like a callus, cold-hearted creep, and when he saw Earlene again, he pretended to have no recollection of what had happened. Thus, there was no apology from him, nor a gram of what could be considered remorse.

So after two or three days of watching that weasel-lollipop around the house like he didn't have a care in the world, something in Earlene's mind just clicked. It told her, "That fool didn't get a punishment—he got a reprieve from justice. Uh, Hun, she said to herself, I knew this was going to happen. And from that moment on, she knew that sooner or later, she would have to deliberate her style of justice.

The two of them were frequently running into each other all through the day. Every time they met, A.J. approached her with a different corny joke, trying to break the ice between them. And in every instance, Earlene told him she didn't want to hear his stupid joke. Even more perplexing was that she didn't have a chance to stomp a mud-hole in his ass on those particular occasions because Grandma was always somewhere nearby with open ears.

Anyway, A. J. couldn't stop being a pest. He was like a junkie, and he had to keep on messing with that girl! One reason why he did it was because of the rejection she dismissed him with. It upset him to the point where—if he couldn't make her laugh; he was going to make her life miserable. And sure enough, A.J. took it to the next level and came up with another plan to piss her off.

He knew that every morning at five o'clock, she'd go to the bathroom. Her routine was like clockwork; it never failed. The loud squeaking noise on the floor coming from the wooden boards would wake him every time she walked down the hall to the bathroom. But this time, he said to himself, I'm going to make that noise stop. It's going to sound a lot different this time. Instead of hearing that squeaking, the floor was going to snap, crackle, and pop!

So later on, on that long, hot, tumultuous night, A.J. went through with his plan to fortify his comedic skill to show her that he was the "King of The House." But what he was doing was opening up an invitation to an ass-whooping. Anyway, this dastardly dude turned his video console up on full blast to drown out the sound of a short-handled rip-saw that he used to cut the floorboard on the second-floor ceiling. He cut half-way through four-wide slats of old rotten wood of the floorboard next to the upstairs bathroom. After that, he went upstairs and placed a furry throw rug over the area he cut.

Then he went to bed. It was up to Earlene to fall into his trap. Six hours later, and as usual, Earlene got up and headed toward the bathroom. And as usual, the squeaking from the floor was back. She walked down to the front of the bathroom door and stepped on the throw rug. It felt good to her bare feet. But as she stood there for a moment, something seemed strange to her. She looked down and saw the throw beneath her feet and got a funny vibe because it hadn't been there before. Nevertheless, she noticed that the squeaking had stopped, but in the split-second that followed, something gave-away. All of a sudden, something snapped, then the floor crackled, and a microsecond later, there was a loud, thunderous POP echoing through the hall.

Earlene fell half-way through the floor up to her elbows and was screaming at the top of her lungs. She was scared to death. Her legs were kicking, twisting, and dangling from the second-floor ceiling. When A. J. heard the noise he laid in in his bed, laughing as he visualized the whole scene.

When he finally got up, he approached the disaster area with caution and looked up at the bottom of Earlene's feet. Then he facetiously asked her: "Damn Earlene, what happened! How in the hell did you get stuck in the floor? Well, anyway, I bet you got time to listen to one of my jokes now, don't you? I got a riddle for you. Listen to this one Earlene: What do you call a monkey walking through a minefield?" But all he could hear was the muffled sound of her cursing like a crazed psychopath.

But being eager to tell her the punchline, he said: "you call it a Baa-Boom! You get it, a Baa-Boom! Ah ha, ha, ha, ha, ha, ha, ha!" And right after he told his corny joke, he added insult to injury; he couldn't resist the temptation to tickle the bottom of Earlene's feet while she was hanging there in limbo. And when he did, she kicked at him and twisted and turned her body from side to side, desperately trying to free herself from that hole in the floor. Her vicious response to him was: "I know you had something to do with this, A. J., and when I catch you, it's All Over For Your ASS"!

So, around about 5:30 that morning, Earlene broke free from her state of temporary incarceration. She held both arms straight up over her head and shoulders and kicked her legs. It was painful, but it worked—she slid through and landed on the floor below. By this time, A J. was nowhere around.

Earlene was enraged. When she got to her feet, she swore that this time, nobody was going to stop her from giving that bicycle stealing, smart-ass little runt the beat-down he deserved.

She was ready for action, she had a plan, and she knew just how to catch that RAT! In short, she enticed him with just the right bait to make him come to her.

She had a grim look on her face, and her motivation was the picture that lingered in her mind of a tombstone in a graveyard with A. J.'s name written on it. To sum it up, at this point, she didn't mind doing time for murder.

Well, it took a while, but Earlene didn't have to wait long at all for that boy to show up. It took her about ten minutes to bait a trap that she knew he was bound to fall in to. She set her trap in the living room by setting out a pitcher of Kool-Aid that Danielle made the night before and some paper cups that Grandma used to make ice-balls.

Then she set it on the cocktail table in the front room and turned the T.V. on. Next, she got one of her Michael Jackson D V D's, put it in the player, and turned up the volume. Then she turned off the lights using the wall switch next to the sofa. Finally, she climbed to the top of the back end of the sofa and stood there in the darkness with a frying pan in her hand and waited for A.J. to hear the music and come through the doorway.

Well, as it turned out, it happened just like she expected. It didn't take long for A.J. to hear the music and come running to the living room. He looked inside and saw the pitcher of Kool-Aid sitting on the table and hesitated for a moment because it was dark inside. But he didn't see Earlene anywhere around, and he couldn't resist the sound of the music, plus he was thirsty. So, at his own risk, he cautiously stuck his head inside and did a quick scan of the furniture to see if anyone was in there. But how he missed seeing those two big bare feet of Earlene's on top of the couch at the end of the room was a marvel in itself.

So, beyond his better judgment, A.J. got Jiggy with it. He started dancing and prancing, finger-popping and booty bopping, unaware of Earlene's stalking presence, high above and behind him. Well, soon afterward, the music sounded so good to him that he forgot all about Earlene chasing him, and he decided that it was refreshment time, and, that's right— "He drank the Kool-Aid." After that, he went right back into his Michael Jackson imitation, and he moon-walked back into the arms of his beholder. Suddenly the lights came on but damned if he saw her coming.

Earlene jumped on that boy's back like she was a cowboy riding a bucking Bronco. She started banging him upside his head with that frying pan, and he fell to the floor with her still on his back. She screamed and shouted at him: "I Got Your Ass Now, Don't I, You Little Creep!" Then she stood up and jumped on that boy's back like it was a trampoline. To top it off, she kicked him in the two major orifices of his body–his big mouth and his little ass.

After that excruciating three-minute bout, an imaginary bell must have rung: Ding, Ding, Ding, because Earlene went to her neutral corner to get her second wind. She had a seat on the couch with A.J. still laying on the floor sprawled out on his belly– petrified and unable to move. He looked like a Pygmy that just got stampeded by a herd of elephants.

The only weapon at his disposal was the telephone lying on the floor in front of him, and he laid there knowing that he had to do something quickly before the bell rang to start round two. So out of desperation, he grabbed the phone and quickly dialed 911.

However, he wanted to save face because he knew Earlene was still in the room listening to him when he picked up the phone, and he didn't want to sound like a punk when he talked to the operator, so he changed the true context of what had happened in the conversation to sound more favorable for him.

Hello, 911 emergency."

"Hello, 911."

"Yes, can I help you?"

"Y'all Better Come Get Her Before I Kill Her!"

"Sir, what's the problem?" How can I help you?

"There's been an Attempt On My Life!"

"What happened, sir?"

"It's my cousin, Earlene. She Dunn went crazy! She jumped on my back, knocked me down, and started beating me in the head with a frying pan. Then she jumped on my back and kicked me everywhere. I'm gonna Kill her if Y'all don't come and get her."

"Well sir, where is she at right now?"

"She's sitting on the couch sipping on a cup of Kool-Aid.

"Well, sir, where are you right now?"

"I'm lying here on the floor with a Knot In My Ass!"

"Sir, are there any weapons in the house?"

"Weapons? No—I don't think so. Oh Yeah! My daddy's "nine"

is around here somewhere, and if I find it, she's gonna have more holes in her than a piece of Swiss Cheese!"

Earlene bolstered with contempt when she heard him say that. She shouted: "Shut up and get off the phone, you little Weasel!" And A.J. was so emotionally charged that his only recourse was:

"Ooow! I'm gonna get you Earlene; I swear I'm gonna get you!"

So, awakened by the distraction coming from the front room was Grandma. She came from her bedroom in the back, and when she saw all the destruction around her and the casualty of war at her feet, she snatched the phone from A.J. Then she started in on both of them. Boy, get your devilish behind off the floor. Earlene, what are you doing down here? Y'all better clean up this mess and be ready for church in the morning!

Lord have mercy, Y'all are going to send me to my grave!" Then she put the phone to her ear to see who was on the other end. "Hello, who is this?" The voice answered: "This is the 911 operator, ma'am. Is everything alright?" "No honey, but it will be, even if I have to find a switch and beat the meat off somebody's behind in here! There's no need for the police; I've got this, honey." "Well, if you need us, give us a call." "Thank you, honey, goodbye."

Ms. Ella had a troubled mind after that, but she still went out of her way to clean up the mess in the living room. And while she was doing that, she looked up at the ceiling and started mumbling these words: "Lord Jesus, I keep telling that boy to leave that girl and her things alone—he just won't listen; he's just too hard headed! I don't know why he keeps on doing the things he does Lord. And Lord, I knew deep in my heart that it was just a matter of time before that girl was going to KICK THAT LITTLE BOY'S ASS!"

CHAPTER TWO

THE "JIG IS UP"

Well, while the flames of fury were boiling down to a simmer on the west side of town. The next order of business was to pick up two feisty fireballs on the east side of town. The history of sibling rivalry between this brother and sister tandem during the past few months has been, to say the least, "Unbelievable."

These two kids were with their Grandmother, as well. They came to stay with her six months ago, but as time went by, there was no mention of their parents' return. Therefore, they quickly turned into two nerve-racking, problematic kids. One day after another, they had been more unbelievable than the next for their Grandmother. But today, she was finally getting a break; this morning, she was getting them ready for an extended leave of absence. Within the next two hours, David and Samantha would be headed to church on a bus with the rest of their cousins.

To summarize, the natural order of the events that led up to the necessity of them being on that bus came about partly due to the destruction of Samantha's birthday party. But it started several months earlier due to the alleged treachery that Samantha imposed on her brother about using up all but a drop of syrup for his pancakes. As a result, it sparked a rivalry that escalated into an all-out -war and a sinister plot by Samantha to transformed her irritating brother into a snowman in the backyard.

However, after his transformation back into a normal human being and a temporary loss of memory, a discovery of facts led him to the proof he needed to re-open a Cold-Case, and it was right on in time to ruin Samantha's birthday party.

A Preponderance of Evidence

David's reappearance had been just as mysterious as his disappearance. Sam and her Grandma had just come through the front door when they heard a loud shriek of terror coming from the backyard. The groundhog burrowing underground and around David's feet had awakened him from his deep sleep. But what made him hysterical was seeing a huge Black-Bird from the corner of his eye perched on his shoulder. It was pecking away at a burnt pancake underneath a pair of sunglasses that were partially covering his eyes.

Well, that's when he set a new Olympic record for the 100-meter dash because when he made eye to eye contact with that bird, he busted out of that suit of snow running like a quarter horse out the gate. Furthermore, if his Grandmother hadn't been there to open the back door at the same time that he was headed towards it, there would have been a new opening right through the middle.

Grandma was shocked when she realized that it was David

who was shot by her at the speed of light. "Holy Jesus and Mary," she shouted. "What in the Devil is going on?" So, she followed him through the house (with Samantha close behind). He was shedding his frozen clothes all over the house– in front of the fireplace in the living room, in the hallway, and finally next to the heat vent on the floor of his bedroom– where he stood with a blanket wrapped around him.

He was shivering from head to toe, his teeth were chattering, and he was mumbling incoherent words– making no sense whatsoever. Nevertheless, Grandma still tried to interrogate him about his whereabouts for the past week. And sure enough, her interrogation was complemented with a strong, Oscar-winning backup performance from Samantha.

Grandma was in disbelief– she couldn't make heads or tells out of what he was saying. However, she noticed that whenever he heard Sam's voice in the background, he became enraged, and he began shouting and repeating the same thing: Sa Sa, Sa—am-k-k-k-kno=kno-s-s! Kk, kk—ill H h-h her. I—I-I I- —Ha-ha-ha h h-ATE—He-he h-h—er!

Grandma just walked away with a puzzled look on her face. The only thing she could do is what she knew how to do best— nurse him back into good health. She fixed him a can of soup, fed it to him, and put him to bed with a lot of warm blankets.

Well, so far, Sam's plot to keep her Grandma from knowing that she knew where David was all along was working. "Agent 007" was always somewhere nearby, tuned into every word that was being said between the two of them. But she knew she had to come up with a new strategy to keep her Grandma from finding out what happened to David for all of that time.

Therefore, the clever junior CIA operative put the wheels in her head in motion. She came up with a plan, and that was to be extra nice to David in the morning and convince him that he had been sick. Her goal was to make him believe that whatever he thought had happened to him was just a bad dream.

So, that night, the "Human Popsicle" tossed and turned in his sleep. He would moan and groan in anguish, and there was an occasional fanatical outburst of screams and yelling from time to time, but Grandma was soon by his side to calm him down.

Well, the next morning, David woke up to the warm rays of sunshine glimmering on his face. He yawned and stretched his arms and legs out wide and sat up in bed and inhaled a deep breath of air and let it out. Then he picked up the smell of pancakes cooking in the kitchen. Ah yes, he thought, he was back in his natural domain, and his thoughts and the feeling in his legs were coming back to normal.

A few minutes later, there was a knock at his door. Samantha busted in and was smiling like "Little Miss Sunshine." She was carrying a plate of pancakes with butter on them and soaked with maple syrup. "Hello, my dear brother, "she said cheerfully, and David was stunned. He could hardly believe his eyes or ears; he was flabbergasted; his mouth opened up wide from shock and the smell of those pancakes, and his bottom lip almost touched his chin.

Anyway, in the back of his mind, he still thought that (after all she did to me, this rotten heifer has the nerve to act like everything is alright). On top of that, she has the gall to be so lively and carefree about it.

He scornfully said, "I didn't say you could come in here." But Samantha ignored the tone of voice and skillfully went to work warming up the cold blood running through his veins; she put on a command performance.

"Have you been having those bad dreams again, David?"

"What! What are you talking about?"

"Grandma says you've been real, real, sick."

"Huh! —I've been what!"

"Oh yeah, David. You had a fever and you've been tossing and turning and hollering in your sleep for over a week now."

"But the last thing I remember is building a snowman in the backyard."

"Yep, and that's when you got sick."

"But something else happened that I can't remember."

"Well, here go your pancakes, David. Grandma made-um especially for you, cause you been sick. I mean really, really, really, really sick!"

He was totally confused now. The bomb she just dropped on him blew his mind, and he didn't know whether to swallow the load of bull she just administered or that delicious stack of pancakes in front of him. But those choices didn't last long, because after thinking about it a moment or two, he gave in; he couldn't wait to start swallowing that delicious stack of pancakes in front of him; he filled his belly and nodded off into another comma-like sleep.

And so far, the plan Sam devised was working like a charm. When Grandma entered the room to talk to him, she was too late.

She still wanted to find out where he had been for all this time, but he was fast asleep. It was all over for that notion. So, she just pulled the cover over the "boy wonder," kissed him on the forehead, and took his dirty dishes to the kitchen.

Well, the days that followed turned into weeks. Samantha kept up her academy award performance, and no one was the wiser. After a while, both David and Grandma had forgotten about what was so important for them to know.

When March 1st rolled around, all the snow had melted, and Samantha was preparing for her birthday party. With all the snow gone, there wasn't much for the snowman architect to do.

Today was Samantha's birthday, and she was anxiously awaiting the arrival of her Grandmother from the store with the party favors and decorations for her birthday party. But, in the meantime, David was still wandering around the house from one window to another–looking outside for enough snow to make a snowball.

This boy had it bad; he had a "Snowman Jones," and watching him go "Cold Turkey" was an awful sight to see.

Anyway, Grandma finally made it home. She came through the door with a bag full of party trimmings and food for the party. They asked David to help with the decorations, but he was too stubborn to help, and he continued to mope around the house in a deep funk–looking out one window and then another, in search of a glimmer of the long-gone snow.

However, in due time, and like a sign from above, he noticed something from the back window. There was a flickering of light coming from a dark object sticking out from the ground. It was right in front of the oak tree in the middle of the backyard, and it brought David's curiosity to a peak. Therefore, he couldn't resist going outside to see what it was.

So, when he reached the oak tree, there they were; his missing pair of sunglasses. They were reflecting the sunlight. But how did they get out here, he thought, and as he got closer, he bent down to pick them up and noticed two foot-prints embedded in the ground in front of the oak tree. Then he saw that they were the same size as his. So, for the sake of curiosity, he put his feet in the prints to see if they were a match. And Bam! They fit so well that it jogged his memory like a bolt of lightning, and the moment of truth arrived!

"Real, real sick"! Yeah, Right," is what he murmured to himself in a sarcastic tone. Then he replayed his memory back to what had happened to him on the day of the snowstorm. He remembered building a snowman in the backyard. He remembered that the weather suddenly changed. He remembered running to the back door to get out of the cold, and he remembered being soaked with the water in the bucket that engulfed his head. But he sure as hell didn't see the baseball bat that swung down from the garage ceiling to rattle his brain to the point where he could remember everything that he just now remembered. But he had a very good idea now. He summed it up with one word—Samantha!

And after figuring out what he just now found out, he was consumed with a strong desire for revenge. Somehow, someway he knew he had to get even with her, and his attitude changed from being a mild-mannered detective to being a devious, underhanded creep. His discovery of evidence demanded immediate satisfaction, and guess who was number one on the receiving end of his hit list—his rotten, calculating little sister.

Anyway, the "ice man" played it cool. He went back in the house with a new attitude; cool, calm, and collected and resumed playing the block-head brother role.

When he went back into the house, his behavior towards his Grandma and Samantha changed from stubborn and selfish to helpful and cooperative. He even offered to help with the party decorations, and that drew suspicion in Samantha's mind. They couldn't figure him out, and Samantha couldn't stop looking at him with an eyebrow raised, wondering what he was up to.

Furthermore, David didn't know exactly how he was going to do it, but the destruction of her birthday party was his major objective. He knew he would have to improvise a plan as he went along, but he was determined to do any and everything possible to get revenge.

CHAPTER THREE

THE COLD-CASE REVENGE

A Mystery Resolved

It didn't take long for Grandma and Sam to put their trust in David. After they had gotten over their suspicious thoughts about him wanting to help, he was hanging up decorations and setting out party hats, whistles, and blowing up balloons. Beyond that, Grandma needed him to get the sheet-cake on the back seat in the car, so she sent him out to bring it in.

When David saw the delicious looking sheet cake on the back seat, he slid it toward him. And when he did, he also saw a brown paper bag with his Grandma's medicine in it. It had turned over and began to spill out. He didn't know what it was until he pulled it out of the bag. The bottle had Milk of Magnesia written on it, and whenever he saw his Grandma drink this stuff, he knew that soon afterward, she'd be running to the bathroom.

He paused for a moment and thought to himself-hum—" This is just the stroke of luck I need! At that moment, the wheels in his head began to spin, and again, out popped those devilish horns.

He added the two together, and it added up three, and in the next few minutes, he carried a white sheet cake, with white icing, covered with white Milk of Magnesia into the house.

Everything was coming together as planned in the house. Samantha was done with her decorations, and Grandma had a pot of hot-dogs simmering on the stove. As for "King Rat," David, he had spread that bottle of Milk of Magnesia on top of that cake so evenly that no one could tell the difference. He was going to make sure that all of Samantha's greedy, creepy, table-rat friends got a good dose of this medicine.

He sat the cake on the dining room table and slowly stepped back. Then he turned around and looked at Samantha with a conniving grin on his face and walked away as cool as a cucumber. Samantha just looked at him, once again, with her eyebrow raised, wondering what he was thinking.

Regardless of her curiosity, Sam realized that the party time was soon approaching, so she hopped to her feet and ran to her bedroom to change clothes. But sooner than expected, and a few minutes after she had finished dressing, the doorbell rang—some of her friends arrived early.

Nonetheless, David was there to greet them at the door, and he was the typical nuisance that he had always been around her friends. He opened the door and looked down his nose at them like they were a group of subhuman species; he cut and rolled his eyes at each member of the rat pack as they came through the door.

The first of her friends to be scoured by his dislike was Fat Elmo. He was about four-feet-two, three-feet-wide, and he would grunt like a pig when he ate. The next goofball through the door was Weird Wayne. He was six-feet tall, weighed 60-pounds, and he smelled like piss.

Following him was that butt digging, four-eyed Fred. He was an average-sized kid for an 8-year old, but he was as blind as a bat; he wore glasses with a quarter-inch thick lens in them, and he still ran into everything. Heading up the rear of the pack was Silly Sarah; she laughed at everything that amused her and everything that distracted everybody else. Then there was Buffy, A.K.A (Scruffy Buffy) always dressed like an old bag-lady and looked like a human Raggedy-Ann doll. Her favorite past-time was picking buggers and eating them when she didn't think anybody was watching her. And finally, there was that big mouth, nerve-racking Talk-a-Lot Tonya. She was the Queen of gossip, and she could talk faster than the speed of sound.

Anyway, just as the front door shut, Samantha's bedroom door opened. She made her grand entrance wearing her new birthday dress and new shoes, and in a matter of seconds, the whole house was filled with laughter from the sound of exuberant children. And within a matter of minutes, the talking, laughing, and yelling got louder and louder. It was so loud in the house that David stuck his fingers in his ears to drown out the noise.

As he was doing so, he walked down the hall to his bedroom to observe the creepy, soon to be funky little kids from the privacy of his bedroom. He couldn't wait for his Grandma to cut that "damned cake" and for Samantha's greedy little friends to start stuffing their faces.

While he was waiting for phase 1 to happen, he started phase

23

2 of his dastardly plan. With music playing, whistles blowing, balloons bursting, and the constant, screeching, high shrill laughter going on, it had gotten to be too much for Grandma as well.

She finally grabbed her dinner bell and rang it desperately to get the kids to shut up, and in the next few moments, she had all the kids sitting at the dining room table in front of the birthday cake. Then she lit the candles on the cake and led them in a chorus of Happy Birthday.

While all of this was going on, her spiteful rat of a brother put his plan into action. From the look of his meticulous handy work, you could tell that he was up to no good. He unscrewed the outside faceplate from the bathroom doorknob; he took it apart and detached the locking mechanism from the inside doorknob; then, he screwed the faceplate back on.

Finally, he slid the outside doorknob back on the stem. The result was a loosely fitted doorknob hanging on the doorknob stem. Furthermore, with the door locked from the inside, no-one could get in without the key he had tied to a shoestring he hung around his neck. Everything was set, so her rat of a brother went to his bedroom across the hall, and all he had to do was sit and wait and watch to see which one of Samantha's funky little friends would be first to run to the bathroom.

Samantha had just blown out the candles on her cake and made her wish. After that, the sound of eight hungry kids, gorging their faces with hot dogs, potato chips, punch, and cake and ice cream was heard for the next thirty minutes—it sounded like feeding time at the zoo.

Likewise, a party of this caliber usually has what is described as a "Table Pimp" to taking charge of the left-over food and such. And two of the most scandalous Table Pimps" east of the Mississippi River were Fat Elmo and Weird Wayne. They were the self-appointed freeloaders of this party, and they had a reputation for being the most astute party going rogues in the neighborhood.

For example, before they had even finished eating, those two scoundrels were fussing about the food they were going to take home with them.

Meanwhile, they filled their bellies and got ready for the real fun that was about to begin. First, they watched Sam open her presents. She got dolls, rollerblades, a CD player, some puzzles, and some board games, and she was happy and delighted with them. But, right after that, Grandma brought out a game that they could all play together. It was called "Twister." It was a game that had a large, thick sheet of plastic covered with multi-colored circular dots.

It had a control board with a direction arrow attached that the players had to spin. Whatever color the arrow landed on would be the spot where the player could place either their hand or foot. The object of the game was for them to all play together without falling.

Grandma got them started with the first spin and showed them how to play it. But soon afterward, after all the stretching and twisting from one color to another, she realized that she wasn't getting any younger and retired for the evening. The kids kept on falling on her tired, aching back, and despite them begging her to stay and play some more, Grandma got off the floor, shook her head, and limped away, rubbing her hip.

On the other hand, David was carefully tuned-in to what was going on in the front room. He had just wolfed down three hot dogs and was patiently waiting for the moment when that mild laxative would have its strong effect. Pretty soon, it would start churning in the bellies of those creeps, and he wanted to see the expression on their faces when they exploded like a volcano in their draws.

Grandma had just passed by his room, headed toward her bedroom, but the party wasn't over yet. The little "hood-rats" were still playing out front, and his party was just about to begin. So, he sat back in his chair, thought of what he'd do when the moment came, and grinned like a Rotten Grinch.

Well, the law of physics states that: "for every action, there is an equal and opposite reaction." But the reaction that came from Samantha's funky friends after eating the laxative on top of that birthday cake was stupendous. It was "more powerful than a locomotive," and it had them ready to leap to the bathroom in a single bound. These kids were not going to forget this birthday party any-time soon.

It was Elmo's turn to play, and Silly Sarah was spinning the dial. It landed on a red dot, which is where Elmo had to place his foot. The closest red dot to him was between Fred and Tonya, but to get to it meant that he had to bring his right leg over the top of Samantha's head and down to the other side of Wayne and straddle his back.

Well, between the time Elmo got his fat leg up and over the top of Samantha's head was when the first explosion erupted.

That fat little kid let out a loud, long explosion of gas that shook the front room window, rattled the dishes in the China Cabinet, and had a smell that could've gagged a maggot.

Anyway, Samantha can thank her lucky stars that she wasn't an inch taller because she probably would have wound up deaf and temporarily blind for the next few months. Instead, the fuming hot gas whizzed across the back of her head and caused the short hair at the base of her neck to stand to attention.

"Ooh! You farted on me, Elmo!" she shouted. Elmo was so embarrassed and blushing so much that his facial expression turned from red to deep purple. And naturally, he lied about it. He shouted: "Unt un! That wasn't me; that was Wayne!"

Nevertheless, a few seconds later, the whole intertwined structure had collapsed, and everyone hit the floor. They were screaming and shouting at each other with fury. Hysteria broke out, and bodies pummeled, stomachs grumbled, and more and more gas rumbled.

Tempers flared and damned if eight-year-old kids didn't know how to swear. They were all guilty of making the house smell like a funk-factory, but they had no idea who the culprit was that made them all loose in the caboose.

After a while, it looked like a thick cloud of gas had filled the room. It smelled so bad that the wallpaper was peeling from the kitchen walls. If there were any flies around, their deaths had to have been quick and painless.

Samantha thought it wise to open the front door to let some

fresh air in, and similarly, David thought it wise to pinch his nose before sticking his head out the door of his room to see what was going on. That's when he saw little, fat Elmo wobbling down the hall to the bathroom.

He hurried to the bathroom door and turned the knob in desperation to get inside. But to his surprise, the knob came off the stem right into his hand. He looked at the knob in his hand, dropped it, and immediately began banging on the bathroom door and hollering at the top of his lungs. All the while, David was standing across the hall, snickering like a circus clown. He took pleasure in watching that little Boy go through his panic attack.

In the same manner, throughout Elmo's twilight zone experience, he felt the eyes of people looking at him from two directions. He looked down the hall and saw the kids watching in silent disbelief, but even more scary was the feeling he got from the eyes of that devilish grin of David's.

And just like that, it was time for David's Grand Finale performance. And with no concern about disturbing his Grandma in her bedroom, he started singing like one of the Temptations.

"Shake Your Ass!-- Shake it Fast!-- Shake Your Ass!--Show Me What Cha Working With!-- Show me What Cha Working With--Shake Your Ass!--Shake It Fast-- Show Me What Your Working With, I said show me What-cha Working With, Fat Boy!"

Then this nutty kid made a Mojo move. He jumped up and did an about-face maneuver in mid-air, landed on his feet, and shook his butt right in front of that little Boy's face.

Elmo was in shock, and during David's performance, he had forgotten all about using the bathroom. But when he finally snapped out of it, he slowly swung his short, stubby arm around to feel his behind and realized that it was too late. There were two pounds of shit in his underwear.

Little Elmo stood there looking pitiful, helpless, and lost. He was so embarrassed that tears started rolling down his face, and then he wobbled to the front room, grabbed his coat, and ran out the door.

Samantha and her friends were standing at the other end of the hallway, watching. They were smitten by David's sudden impromptu performance and by his humiliation tactic. And by now, every rug-rat in the house felt the full effects of the laxative that they unknowingly gobbled down.

David showed them the only key to the bathroom on a shoestring tied around his neck to make his point. Even more noticeable was the way he kept tossing the bathroom doorknob in the air like a baseball. That sight let them know that it was all over as far as using the bathroom in that house. So, they grabbed their coats and ran out the front door like rats jumping from a sinking ship.

Everyone, but Samantha. She stood her ground right where she was and squared off with David. She was at one end of the hallway, and he was at the other end. It was like a scene right out of a Western. "The Good, the Bad, and How in Hell do I Get in the Damn Bathroom."

All of a sudden, Samantha shouted: "Give me that doorknob, David!" David Calmly said: "Unt un," and continued tossing the doorknob in the air like a baseball. Samantha shouted again: "Give it to me, Punk!" David smiled graciously, and in another mellow tone, he said: "Nope." Then she yelled at the top of her lungs," Grandma!" But Grandma didn't budge.

As far as they knew, she was still in her bedroom, sleeping. Then David took the sunglasses from his back pocket and held them out for Samantha to see, and he asked her: "Do you know where I found my sunglasses?" Samantha's quick, smart-aleck response was: "Yeah, on a store Dummy, Dummy!" David just smiled, shook his head, and said, "Unt un."

And incredibly, the next move Samantha made went by so fast that the only way anyone could have seen it is on an instant replay camera. She streaked down the hall like a flash of light, kicked David in the leg, caught the doorknob in mid-air, and put it on the stem, and tried to open the door. But she couldn't open it because it was locked from inside. And now, being angry as ever, she turned around to see David dangling the bathroom key on that shoestring in the air high above her head.

By this time, neither one of them noticed Grandma peeping at them from around the corner, and Samantha leaped and leaped and leaped for that key and couldn't reach it. Then she kicked and kicked and kicked at David's legs to get him to drop the key until, Oops—it happened! Samantha suddenly realized what she had done–she had a big pile of party poop in her panties, and it was running down the back of her leg.

She let out a loud, sorrowful cry sobbing like a baby. She shouted with tears in her eyes, "Grandma!"

Once again, David couldn't resist rubbing salt in the wound of this humiliating situation. The Rap-star was compelled to do his final performance one more time. So, wasting no time at all, he started singing: Shake Your Ass!-- Shake it Fast!-- Shake Ya Ass! But, unfortunately, that's as far as he got.

All of a sudden, there was a loud noise that sounded like gunfire-- KA-POW—Then a painful sounding "AHHH.. ... SHIT" came out of David's mouth. He looked behind him and saw his Grandma standing there holding a thick, leather razor strap, and this time, Grandma shouted: "SHOW ME WHAT YA WORKING WITH!" And Damned if he didn't! All she could see was ass and elbows. He showed her what he was working with alright. He ran out the front door like a fugitive from justice. So, Grandma just stood at the front door and watched him for a while. He hid behind cars, trees, houses, and even underneath a man-hole cover. Then she shouted, "BOY, DON'T LET ME CATCH YOUR ASS IN THE STREET!"

CHAPTER FOUR

ROAD TRIPPING

The Mission Begins

Grandma Williams and Grandma Walker were themes of the same variation. In the past, the more crap a child got away with was equally proportionate to the punishment they'd receive—if not more. They both believed in family values and old school discipline.

Anyway, it was time to go. Samantha looked up at her Grandmother with sad eyes and said, "I'm going to miss you Grandma." David spoke his heart as well. "I'm going to miss you too Grandma." Then they both put their arms around her and held her tight. Grandma welled up inside, and her voice was filled with sadness when she said. "I'm going to miss you babies too."

Then Samantha backed away, and sobbing and trembling with fear; she said, "I love you Grandma." Grandma said, "I love you too Samantha." Then, she ran to her Grandma again, wrapped her arms around her waist, and held on to her tight. So, Grandma held her head to her bosom, stroked her hair, and soothed away her fear. "Come on now, she said. We'll be back together soon. The time will just fly by. You and David will have so much fun that you won't even miss me, and I'll call you in a few days to see how you're doing, O'K, I promise."

After hearing that, Samantha was relieved. She wiped the tears from her face and gave her Grandma a big smile. Then she said, O'K, Grandma, I'll be waiting for you to call. Then Grandma stood at the front door and watched them walk to the bus. As David was getting on the bus, she noticed he was wearing that same pair of raggedy gym-shoes, but it was too late to stop him– he was already on the bus. He slapped Alvin a high-five and immediately ran to the back of the bus to sit with A.J. Nevertheless, Alvin stepped off the bus and spoke to her. "Hi, Aunt Jan," and she responded, "High, Alvin. Hey Alvin, will you make sure that boy puts on his good pair of shoes before he gets to church? "No problem, Auntie, I will." "You all have a good time, and be careful driving, Alvin."

Well, as soon as Samantha got on the bus, she found the nerve to square off with Alvin. She got to the top step two feet in front of his face and said, "you heard my Grandma! You better drive this bus like you got some sense, and Don't be Speeding!" But coming from a family with five sisters, Alvin refused to be intimidated. So, he eased back in his seat, looked her up and down, and told her to go sit her little Peter Pan ass down so he could drive the bus. Then, he started the bus and mumbled some profound words. Samantha heard him say: (I'm on a mission from God!). An exasperating, "Oh Boy," came from her mouth, along with a look at him like he was a nut. Then she strolled down the aisle to the back of the bus.

Although this was the first time David met A.J., they took to each other like fish to the water. Within minutes of talking, A.J. had dubbed David with the alias D.A. due to his middle name (Alafia). Earlene, Tamara, and Danielle were all sitting in the middle seats. They were gabbing on and on about all the things they were going to do this summer. But when Samantha reached them, she was timid and shy. She was the youngest member of the bunch; however, they all took the time to welcome her with open arms to ease her.

Meanwhile, as they all prepared to get comfortable, they looked toward the front and saw Alvin pop a tape in his cassette player. Then he stuck a pair of earbuds in his ears and put on his sunglasses. That's when the first thought crossed their mind that they better get ready for the wildest bus ride of their lives.

Grandma Williams was still at the front door with a bewildered look on her face. She was trying to figure out where she saw that raggedy-ass bus before. Then it came to her–it was the same broken down jitney that was in the empty lot next to her sister's house.

She busted out laughing and started talking to herself. (lord, somebody must have been doing a whole lot of praying, she thought. Because whatever they did to get that thing up and running was short of a miracle).

Anyway, Alvin had been a metro-city bus driver for twenty years and knew all the city streets, back-alleys, shortcuts, and where all the main potholes were like he knew the back of his hand. But he still had one vice—listening to James Brown while he was driving. He'd put on his music to drown out everything and everybody around him, and listening to James Brown was the stimulus that aroused his soul and allowed him to "Get on the Good-Foot," and likewise, it triggered his reckless style of driving.

The task ahead for Alvin was a big one. He had to make several more stops until he picked up everyone on his list. That meant traveling from one neighborhood to another all around the city.

Therefore, after he buckled his seat belt, put on his sunglasses, and popped a James Brown tape in his cassette player, he "Got on the Good foot. He popped the clutch and took off like he was coming out of a pit-stop at the Indy-500. He drove up the street and down to the bottom of Sheffield Road in a matter of seconds.

When he reached the bottom, there was a 25mph speed limit sign, so he came to a complete stop to observe the landscape. There was a long winding road with fenced-in pastureland on both sides of the road ahead of him. The reason for the fence was that there might be a few dozen heads of cattle grazing at any given time. Now and then, the cattle would get spooked by the sound of loud cars and trucks passing by and go astray—at times trampling over the fence and winding up on the road. Furthermore, on this particular morning, there was a thick fog hovering over the road ahead.

A little way down the road, he spotted a cow in the middle of the fog-filled road, then another and another. And despite these kids' fear, protesting, and hollering at him to not do what he was obviously going to do, it was useless. They realized that he had those earbuds stuck in his ear. He couldn't hear a word they were saying. He was tuned in and turned on to James Brown so much that nothing else mattered.

Regardless of the situation, Alvin perused the road ahead, and sure enough, he took off like a kamikaze pilot on a search - destroy mission.

He turned on his bright lights, blew his horn, and with his mind being absorbed with the thought of completing the mission he set out to do, he continued driving with reckless abandon. These kids had no other recourse except to respond in unison with a long, drawn-out: AWE … … … … … … … … SHIT!

He zig-zagged his way through a milelong stretch of cows and cow manure in less than 10 seconds. He swerved left in front of the first cow and grazed its jaw, making it turn around and go back to the field that it came from. He broke to the right of the second cow and ran over a huge pile of cow manure. All of a sudden, the rear end of the bus fishtailed one-way, then the other, and it just so happened that the back end of the bus smacked a cow on its rear end and pushed it across the road into the field on the other side of the road.

Several yards later, he saw two more cows crossing the road. One was behind the other with about three yards between them, and he immediately mashed on the accelerator and shot right between them like he was in a demolition derby. The two cows scampered away in different directions only to wind up, falling over in the ditches on the sides of the road.

Then he got to a bend in the road and couldn't see around the corner. A cow was standing in the middle of the road. It was mooing and seemed to be mesmerized by the bus engine's sound and the oncoming light in the street. Alvin slowed down a little, but he was still traveling a little too fast when he saw the cow standing there. He quickly hit the breaks to avoid hitting it, but by now, his front and back tires were covered with cow manure, and the bus skidded several feet before Alvin could get control of it, and as a result, the bus went into a 360 degree flat spin. Bodies pummeled and tumbled from one side of the bus to the other; they spent completely around in a circle in the middle of the road before they came to a stop.

Anyway, after they stopped spinning, Alvin got his bearings together and made a U-Turn. He drove off the road into the grass. Then he drove right past the cow that was miraculously still standing in the same spot and got back on the road.

Well, when they finally reached the end of the road, there was a sigh of relief. The Holy Crusaders had made it this far, but there were a few more stops to make before they reached the church. Consequently, all of them were seriously wondering if they would make it there before they met their maker.

They were at the intersection of the main road, where they made a right turn and rode a half-mile to the first light. Then, they made a left turn onto Route 42 and followed it down a hill—up a hill—and down another hill until they reached the I-75 entrance ramp and merged into the highway traffic. Not more than three minutes later, he got off at the Lincoln Heights exit and went straight to big mama's house, where three more cousins were waiting: Leroy, Sparkle, and Leon.

Leon alone was a nerve-racking nuisance. And their mother had to deal with daily problems that involved keeping him from staying high on pot all day, keeping Leroy out of jail from selling crack, and keeping Sparkle away from a hot-tail group of girls who would do any and everything to get money. Other than that, keeping a steady job and enough food in the house was a day to day concern.

Anyway, after he picked them up, he drove to the upper sub to pick up cousins Lee, his sister, Lavada, and Alvin's favorite cousin, Little Gary—AKA-Popsicle. But first, he took a short ride through the hood to see how much things had changed, and where he encountered several amusing situations.

The first sight was a group of angry people shouting and cursing at the police. They called them a bunch of no good ass crooks on the take. Alvin heard some of the conversations and kept on driving, saying that some shit never changes. In most cases, the cops would harass the dope boys, take their drugs, take their money, locked them up, and let them out the next morning. That was standard procedure and the modus operandi of the LHPD. Most of the time, the police had more drugs to get high on and sold more drugs than the local dope boys.

As he drove further up the street, and before he could turn the corner, he almost ran into an old wino who walked out in the middle of the road. He forced Alvin to make a sudden stop. And after he stopped, the man banged on the hood of the bus and shouted, "What's my name, God-dammit." He stood there mumbling with his body weaving back and forth, saying the same thing over and over. Then he stared inside the bus with a frightful look on his face. But Alvin knew the from a long time ago, so he got off the bus and helped the man to the curb where he sat him down. Then Alvin reached in his pocket and handed the man a few dollars. He used to be a brilliant architect and a brick mason back in his day. He had built nursing homes and houses throughout the city, but for some reason, he lost his mind, and he set fires to the places he would build before he even finished them.

Anyway, after that, he drove midways down the hill to the Valley Homes–the projects where Popsicle lived. And as soon as they turned the corner, they saw the cherry-lipped bandit. Alvin spotted him in the parking lot shaking a pair of dice. He got the nickname Popsicle because when he was younger, his mother spoiled him rotten. Whenever she took him to the corner store, he would beg, cry, whine, and demand that she buy him a Popsicle. And if she didn't, he'd pitch a bitch-fit. He'd lay down in the middle of the floor kicking and crying until she or someone did–sometimes even strangers would buy him a popsicle to shut him up.

Anyway, Alvin pulled in the parking lot and saw him in a crap game with five older boys. He was in the middle, down on one knee with his hand raised in the air shaking a pair of dice, swearing to send all of them home broke. So, he threw the dice, and when they landed, his heart sunk. "Snake eyes, sorry little nigga, you lose!" the boys laughed and teased him relentlessly. They told him to: "take your young, broke black-ass home, and don't go away mad, just go the fuck away—you little bastard!"

Popsicle was pissed, in more ways than one. He had just lost all his money, and the lesson in humility that came from those boys sure as hell didn't help his self-esteem.

Well, as it turned out, there couldn't have been a better time for Popsicle to pull off what he did next. Popsicle went into a tirade and started cussing and fussing at everybody around him.

He went wild– jumping up and down on top of the money and kicking it all around. They all thought he had lost his mind. But his next move was unbelievable. All of a sudden, he fell on top of the money, but when he got up, he had a hand full of bills, and he stampeded his way through those older boys like a Heisman Trophy winner.

Alvin had just turned the bus around and was headed back out the parking lot when he saw Popsicle kicking up rocks running away from that mob of thugs. Suddenly, one of the boys caught up with him and grabbed him by the collar of his shirt and held on, but Popsicle changed gears on the boy and came straight out of that shirt. In that same moment, Alvin opened the door to the bus, and Popsicle dove through the bus doors like he was making an endzone play. And he leaped so far that he wound up laying across Alvin's lap.

Alvin's timing was perfect, but when he pulled the door shut, those boys were still running alongside the bus, banging on the door, trying to pry it open. So, Alvin went to work, putting his years of driving skills to good use. He mashed the gas pedal and made an impossible 45 degree turn out of that parking lot. He was traveling so fast, and the turn was so sharp that the bus tilted on two of its side wheels going around the corner.

Well, they got away, but not before the back of the bus was bombarded by rocks, bottles, and sticks, and anything that they could find to throw at it. And while everyone on the bus was terrified, Popsicle was happy and as relieved as a convict that just made parole; he narrowly escaped another near-death beat-down. That being the case, he ran to the back of the bus and taunted them through the window. They couldn't hear him, but they sure as hell knew what he was saying. "Y'all some Busters, you can't catch me, Y'all some chumps!" Then he did the cabbage patch— pausing now and then in the middle of his dance to blurt out: "You Can't Touch This."

Well, Despite the jeopardizing situation Popsicle put them through, Alvin had one more stop to make in this wacky city, and he knew it would have to be a quick one. He drove back to the upper sub to pick up Big Lee and Lavada in the nick of time, and they were more than ready to go. The next-door neighbors had just called the police because of all the noise; Lee had just blinded his stepdaddy with an ass-whooping. This stout fifteen-year-old boy was tired of seeing his mother with black eyes every time he came home drunk. And he was tired of him terrorizing his baby sister, so his pint up hostility finally came to a boiling point, and he exploded. Therefore, they were ready to go with their bags packed as soon as Alvin drove up.

Alvin fled from the scene just as the police were arriving. He eventually got back on the freeway and headed straight to his sister Lorraine's house. Then got off the highway and stopped at the red light at the intersection. But when he took off again, they heard the sound of something tapping at the back of the bus. Alvin looked through the side-view mirror and saw his bald, melon head nephew on his bicycle in the middle of the street; he was hanging onto the side of the bus.

Monty was up to his dangerous games again, and not only did he get their attention, but he also got the attention of the semi-truck driver in the left lane coming straight towards him. The driver didn't have much time to make a complete stop, so he started blowing his horn from a block away. Suddenly, Alvin decided to speed up and make a right turn instead of going straight. A split second later, Monty grabbed hold of the bus and followed it out of the path of the oncoming truck, but little did he know that his mother almost had a heart attack watching the whole incident from her porch on the next street.

That was a close call for Monty because if Alvin hadn't made that right turn, he would have wound up lying next to a grease spot in the middle of rode. Nevertheless, he was about to reap the benefit of his good luck in exchange for a sore ass when he got home.

When the bus pulled in the yard, Monty was right behind it on his ten-speed. And when Lorraine spotted him, she immediately did a two-handed vault off the front porch railing into the yard and went straight to where he was standing. He laughed and joked with Earlene and A.J. through the bus window when she shocked the shit out of him. She immediately started beating him with the hard rubber house slipper she pulled off her foot.

Monty tried to bob and weave and cover-up from the stinging blows she was hitting him with. She hit him upside his head and all over his body with that slipper, and she was too damn mad and too damn fast with that slipper to let any open area of contact on his body go unpunished.

The kids on the bus started out feeling sorry for him when they saw the merciless beating he was getting. They couldn't help from cringing and squinting their eyes every time they heard the

43

solid sound of those smacks to his body. However, what came out of his mouth next changed all of that.

After what seemed like an eternity, Monty made the mistake of calling her the "B" word. He must have been delirious from the ass whooping she was putting on him and so fed up with all the licks to his head that he shouted: "Stop hitting me bitch!" Well, the fickle finger of fate changed everything because the sympathy they once had for the num nut turned into instructions on how to beat his ass.

A.J. Hollered out the bus window, "Hit him again, Aunt Lorraine, show him what ya working with."

Earlene Hollered, "Yeah, hit that fool again, Aunt Lorraine. Knock the meat off his off his ass! He needs his ass whooped!"

D.A. said: "You need to use a night-stick on his Ass."

Danielle said: "Yeah, knock the taste out of his mouth, Aunt Lorraine. He ain't got no business cussing at you."

Sam and Sparkle got in on the act, and both of them shouted out the window at the same time, "Yeah, Kick his ass."

Leon heard everything they said and couldn't think of a thing to say, so he just said, "Yeah, what they said. Ehee, heeheeheeheehee."

Anyway, right after that devastating beat-down, they gather up what was left of Monty, got him on the bus, and continued the mission. This time, instead of getting on the highway, Alvin took a shortcut. He went straight down Paddock Road, which took him about ten minutes to get to sister Norlene's house. Once there, he would pick up Big Kim, Ernie, and baby sister Angie.

When he pulled up, they were standing at the door—well dressed, ready to go, and looking very sophisticated. So, with

Alvin pressed for time, they said their goodbyes and got on the bus without delay.

Well, Alvin had one more stop to make before he could head to the church. That stop was the Greyhound station downtown. Little Walter–AKA-Chunk was riding the bus up from Atlanta, and hopefully, he'd be there right on time to pick him up. And as such, he was. The bus had just dropped him off.

From there, they traveled West through a downtown portion of the city to Vine Street. They made a right turn and went up Vine to Mulberry—one of the city's steepest hills. It took a while with the bus filled and luggage everywhere, but that yellow, rusty little jitney bus performed like "The little engine that could." It smoked and choked. Stuttered, and puttered and backfired, until it made it to the top of that hill to the church.

CHAPTER FIVE

A TASTE OF HOLINESS

The elderly Mrs. Walker stood tall and proud when Alvin and the kids pulled up in the bus. But she was shocked when it departed because more than half of them felt a need to show their natural survival instincts. As soon as Alvin pulled off in the bus, there was a loud KA-POW and a Boom. The exhaust system backfired, and they immediately hit the ground like they were in a war zone.

The church members were stunned when they saw their reaction, and Mrs. Walker was slightly baffled herself, but she understood their sudden reaction and told them to "Get up off the ground, ain't nobody shooting at you." Soon afterward, she had them inside the church sitting in the front section of the pews she had reserved.

She had everybody situated and seated in a spot where they could hear the Reverend speak. Everybody, except for Ernie. He had another plan, and that plan was to Mack" Peaches–the Reverend's daughter. He saw her and was attracted to her like a magnet. And from that moment on, he was on the prow.

He walked up to her and said, "Hey girl, I'm Ernie. Can I ask you a question? How long did that trip take?" Peaches just stood there with a puzzled look on her face, but she eventually replied: "What trip?" Ernie looked at her and said: "That trip from Heaven, all the way down here to Earth; you look like an Angel, Baby." Peaches was so tickled that she smiled and busted out laughing and said: "boy, you so silly!" Then Ernie asked for her name and phone number. But, being coy, she just smiled, turned away, and walked towards the front of the church.

But seeing her smile was all the ammunition he needed. His nose was wide open, and he wasn't about to give up now. He followed her to the front of the church and sat down beside her in a pew where they talked for a while. And whatever he said to get her undivided attention must have been spellbinding because, a minute or two later, she dug down in her purse for a pencil and paper, wrote her phone number on it, and handed it to him.

Meanwhile, as the excessive sound of chatter and bantering filled the room, Reverend Kimble made his way to the pulpit to welcome everybody to the church. So, to quiet them down, when he reached the microphone, he spoke loud and clear.

"Can everybody say, Amen?"

The church said: "Amen!"

"I said, can everybody say, Amen!"

"Amen, Reverend; Amen, Amen ..."

"Hallelujah! Praise the Lord! I see the glory of the Lord in church this morning. Oh, Happy Day! I see the Johnson family here. The Thomas family—Alberta and Calvin and their lovely children, praise the Lord, and Sister Walker—my, my, my, it looks like Sister Walker brought her entire family here this morning. Praise the Lord. I see your son Alvin and his children, and I see your other Grandchildren. And these other children must be your brother and sister's, children."

"They're my Great-nieces and nephews Reverend," she said proudly. "Have Mercy, Sister Walker, you must be a Shepherd for the Lord! Yes, truly a Shepherd for the Lord. Everybody, give Sister Walker a round of applauds, Amen."

Nevertheless, the family acknowledgments kept coming from the Reverend as he noticed several other new members of the church. But, as time went by, he got lost in his thoughts, and his words and the meaning behind them began to carry mixed messages. It was obviously due to the distractions that had him gazing in the front pews below him. Several young women were sitting in the front pews provocatively dressed with their legs crossed. Furthermore, they wore tight-fitting, short cut dresses and had on tight silk blouses to accentuate their breast and the curves in their bodies.

On several occasions, Mrs. Kimble—who was also the organist, played a loud, long screeching note on the organ to let him know that his comments were out of line. Whenever he heard those long screeching notes on the organ, it made him nervous and caused him to perspire. Therefore, he was constantly pulling the handkerchief from his back pocket to wipe the sweat from his face and forehead.

Anyway, it just so happened that these young women in the front pews knew just what they were doing, and it didn't stop them from purposely performing their act of effrontery. Furthermore, they got a kick out of seeing the Reverend squirm and sweat like the adulterating creep he truly was. Besides that, they wanted to show the Reverend's wife that he was a two-faced snake and a womanizing creep.

So, the Reverend hurried to finish his acknowledgments, because he knew that his lust filled roaming eyes were getting him in deep trouble with his wife– not to mention the elder members of the congregation. Their disdain showed on their facial expressions. So, with no further ado, the Reverend stuttered and stammered his final remark: "Everybody have a blessed and booty-full day."

That was the mouthful that made Mrs. Walker hold her head down and shake it back and forth, murmuring to herself: (My mama always said he was a weasel).

Nevertheless, it was time for sister Althea to announce the Sunday morning itinerary. So, feeling the embarrassment of her husband's blundering remark, she reluctantly approached the podium. Until this point, the kids had been quiet and peaceful, but now they were getting restless. They had no interest in what Reverend Kimble or his wife was saying. Their main interest was in observing members of the opposite sex and cracking jokes about anybody that amused them. And at that moment, listening to Sister Althea speak bored them to the end of their wits. They were hot and thirsty, and their backsides ached from sitting on those hard, wooden pews. They were ready to get up and bust a move or do something.

Fortunately, relief came just in time. Sister Althea finished her announcements, and they all broke up into Sunday school groups. They all dispersed upstairs and downstairs in the basement.

Tables and chairs were set up in the basement of the church, and the number of groups was determined by the deacons and elders of the church. So, after a few minutes of careful yet speedy calculations, appropriate decisions were made as to who and how many people would be in the groups.

As it turned out, A. J., D. A., Leon, Popsicle, and Monty were all in one group. Ernie, Lee, Leroy, Walter, and a few other kids were in another. And the girl groups included: Earlene, Samantha, Danielle, Lavada, and Sparkle in the same group, and Kim Angie and Tamara were upstairs in another.

Furthermore, there were so many people in attendance that week that Reverend Kimble had his daughter, Peaches, teach one of the groups. That group just happened to have the five Rambling Rascals in it. Also, twin sisters—Jeanie and Janie, AKA the X-Ray Vision sisters, were in it. The boys referred to them with this name because of the thickness of the lens in their glasses. And there was another boy in their group named, Antwone; AKA 'Precious', whom the boys made fun of because of his soft feminine voice.

With the situation being what it was, Peaches told them that her lesson for the week would be about Jonah and the Whale.

The next group was headed up by Sister Althea–the Reverend's wife. She was a nice-looking woman in her mid-fifties, but she was also a stern and uncompromising woman who demanded respect. Her group included Ernie, little Walter, Leroy, Lee, and five sassy girls with snobbish attitudes and chips on their shoulders. Their subject matter was about the trials and tribulations of Job.

Deacon Brown was the mentor in charge of the group with Earlene, Samantha, Danielle, Lavada, and Sparkle. They were sitting next to four boys whose uncouth behavior and their unsavory smell made them sick. They stunk in every way imaginable. They had terrible breath, funky underarms, and they wore second-hand clothes that smelled like they came off a garbage truck. Deacon Brown had his hands' full heading up this group. And it was just a matter of time before it spontaneously combusted like fireworks. Their discussion today was the story of Sampson and Delilah.

Big Kim, Angie, and Tamara were reluctant to sit with a group of girls whose understanding of the Bible was a lot different than theirs. Therefore, there was a combination of righteous indignation and contempt between them about religious issues. That brought out the worse in these girls, and as a result, their disagreements led to a 'Bible Thumping Calamity.' Their mentor, Sister Pauline, did her best to maintain peace and order between these girls misconstrued conception by citing the actual scripture from the Bible about the Descendants of Abraham.

Anyway, Peaches started telling her group the story about Jonah and the whale; however, when she got to the part about Jonah being tossed in the sea and swallowed by a whale, it was too hard for them to believe. As a result, with them being the smart asses they were—they adamantly questioned and criticized her information: (How could a man be swallowed by a whale and come out alive three days later). Disbelief was in their minds, and their imaginations were set on a course of ridiculous questions, comments, and jokes that perpetuated laughter throughout her lesson. Their inquisition of ignorance went as such:

Monty said: "Hey A.J., what would you do if you got swallowed by a whale?"

A.J. said: "man, if a whale swallowed me, I'd pull out my nine and shoot it in the ass until it opened up its mouth and let me out."

D.A. said: "If a whale swallowed me, I'd start cooking his ass from the inside out. Then i'd put some hot sauce on it and eat me a big ass fish sandmich."

Monty said: "Yeah, but then you'd want some coleslaw and a bottle of coke to go with it?"

Popsicle: put his hand in his back pocket where he kept his knife and said, "I'd Fillet his ass. He'd be fried, died, and laid to the side when I'm through him." The only thing I'd want to go with it is some French fries."

Leon thought about what Popsicle said and instantly blurted out: "Yeah, and some ketchup. Eeeh-hee hee hee hee hee.Eeeh-hee hee …!"

Twin sisters Jeanie and Janie had heard the story before, and they tried to tell the five stooges about the message in it, but they got shot down every time they tried. They had had enough. It wasn't worth their time to explain to those jackasses the lesson in the story. And Precious just quietly sat there shaking his head back and forth in disbelief. He wasn't about to say a word in favor of or against the discussion.

Nonetheless, from the corner of his eye, Ernie could see that Peaches was struggling with the nonsense that his cousins were taking her through. Occasionally she caught a glimpse of him watching her, and the only way she could communicate to him was with the excruciating smile on her face—which let him know that he was still in the running for her affection. She bravely continued to tell the story, with Jeanie and Janie being her only listening pupils.

But, as they continued, A.J. noticed that Antwone was staring at the ceiling with a smile on his face and was curious about why he was doing it. So, he asked him where his mind was and what he was thinking about. Nevertheless, still smiling, Precious nonchalantly answered, "Oh nothing."

Well, Popsicle was wondering the same thing. So, he stared at him for a long, hard minute or two, and he looked up at the ceiling where Antwone was looking, then back at Antwone. Then he turned back around and surmised his assumption to the rest of the boys. He said: "I don't know what he's looking at, but he's got that I want to suck Moby Dick's, Dick look in his eye if you ask me. D.A. immediately responded and said: "You better let him use your knife then, Pop. He's gonna have to cut both corners of his mouth to get that big muthafucka in it.!" Eeeh-hee hee hee hee--Eeeh-hee hee hee--Eeeh-hee hee hee hee ...!"

.

Sister Althea's group got along fine. She found out that Ernie was a well-versed student of Bible scripture, and halfway through the lesson, she let him take control of the group, in which he told the story of Job. He explained that: "Job was a loyal servant to God, and God let the Devil test Job to prove his loyalty to God. And Job proved his loyalty even when his wealth, worldly possessions, and his family members were taken from him. So, the devil lost the bet, and God blessed Job with twice as much as he had before. When Lee figured out the meaning of the story, he said, "I see. It was a test of faith. Job may have lost a lot, but in the end, he gained a lot more because he never gave up his faith in God."

On the other hand, Chunk's academic knowledge was elsewhere. The only thought that crossed his mind was that (The story sounds like God and the Devil were a couple of bookies. And for some reason, Leroy could care less. His mind was on making money, and money was all that was on his mind. He just wanted to get the hell out of there.

Anyway, as the discussions progressed, and at times digressed from the intended lesson, the Rambling Rascals were wandering off—one by one. They were going to the bathroom and disappearing out the basement door. And, with less tension to deal with, Peaches was relieved when she saw them leaving; she didn't care at all. There was less confusion in the group, and it was a lot easier to manage; however, during the next ten minutes, she looked around, and all five of them were gone.

All of them followed the same escape route. The boys went to the bathroom and then out of the basement door next to the kitchen. They went up a long flight of steps to the front of the church and down the steep hill to the store on the corner where they all met.

This was a regular routine for A.J. when he went to church with his Grandma. If he got too bored, he'd slip away and go on a candy run down the hill. Anyway, A.J. had been in the same spot for several minutes before the others showed up. Nevertheless, they all made it. And before long, all five of these knuckleheads were crossing the downtown intersection, headed toward the West End of town.

However, amazingly, it just so happened that the further they walked, the more they felt the strange feeling that someone was watching them or that there was some invisible force field around them. Still, none of them ever mentioned it, and they didn't give it any serious thought. Nevertheless, they felt invincible, and they paraded through the side alleys and downtown streets like a band of gypsies.

Several minutes later, they were in Washington Park, and when they got there, people were sleeping on benches and cardboard boxes. Some younger kids had a game of basketball going on while others watched from the sideline. Across the street, old winos and drug addicts were hanging out in front of a store, panhandling for change.

Further on down the street, the drop-in center had just put a bunch of people out so they could clean up. In the meantime, some of them would wind up in a crap game in an alley and sometimes turn-up shot, stabbed, or dead.

Meanwhile, back at the church, Mrs. Walker and her peers, Sister Wilson, Deacon Bradley, and Reverend Kimble, engaged in a discussion with little to do, and everything to do with the church. They talked about the lack of respect kids today had for themselves and other people. And about the disproportionate number of young black men in jail and the growing number of teenage girls who had become mothers and high school dropouts.

On the other hand, Lee, Ernie, Walter, and Leroy had finally got Sister Althea to stray from the Bible study subject about Job, and they all, including Sister Althea, wound up talking about food, sports, and the opposite sex.

Peaches and her group were getting along fine now that she didn't have to put up with the 'mod squad.' She reported them MIA to the head Deacon about a half-hour earlier, but she had serious doubts about anything being done about it. And with time ticking away, Sunday school was about over. Reverend Kimble was gearing up for his sermon for the week and anticipating the donations from the circulation of the collection plate. Other than that, there were no major concerns at this time.

However, a more critical issue had come up with the girls. Earlene and Danielle were getting pissed off with the disrespect and foul language coming out of the boys' mouths in their group. Sampson and Delilah's story was the Bible lesson in their study group, but their real problem boiled down to the boys defending Sampson and dishing Delilah. The boys despised Delilah, and it became apparent from the language they used to describe her.

They took it as a personal assault against them and to all women. Therefore, they felt compelled to do something about it, so they swore that the next time they called Delilah out of her name–shit was going to hit the fan.

Also, the group's mentor, 80- year- old Deacon Brown was hard of hearing, and at times he suffered from a mild case of dementia. His memory would come and go, and some of the words he heard were hard for him to discern. And with that being the case, these boys exploited the fact of his illness and got away with calling Delilah vulgar names such as: (A medieval prostitute, an ancient Ho, and a double-crossing, backstabbing bitch).

Well, as it turned out, they continued taking turns reading the story out loud, and the boys started talking about Delilah again.

This time one of them called her Rotten Ass Bitch, and before he could get another word out, Earlene jumped up and popped him in his mouth. He went down for the count, but Earlene was still on top of him, hollering: "Your Mama's a Rotten Bitch! You stinky-ass little boy!" Then she sat on him and knocked his head from east to west with right and left hooks.

Fortunately, Deacon Brown glanced over and saw them on the floor in a brawl and snapped back to reality. And it took Deacon Brown with the help of Danielle and Samantha to pull her off him. After the fight, Deacon Brown nervously fumbled through his jacket pocket to find his pills. He quickly swallowed one, and without thinking about where he was, he shouted: "I am too Damn Old for this Shit!" After that, the girls were sent back upstairs to be under Mrs. Walker's supervision.

Earlene knew from the look on her grandmother's face that she wasn't pleased. And as such, she directed all chastisement at her, "Earlene, what happened downstairs? Girl, why are you always fighting?" "Grandma, those rotten boys were calling us names, and I put a stop to it, that's all." "Earlene and the rest of you hear this and hear it well, there is to be no more fighting here in church. If anybody is bothering you, let one of the elders in the church know, or come and tell me. Is that understood?"

"Yes Mam, but Deacon Brown was there and he didn't do anything." "Don't worry about him, you just get up and come and get me! Got it!" "Yes, mam."

Back in the Hood, trouble was in line for these boys, and a clear element of danger was ahead of them. However, regardless of that being the case, these boys still found things in common with the people around them.

D. A. was interested in the basketball game that was going on in the park. And, he got a chance to play and show off his prowess. Although he was good and knew it, he was also a ball hog and tended to piss-off his teammates as well as his opponents.

It was just a matter of time before Popsicle heard the hustle and bustle of a crap game going on in the alley, and the money-hungry, cash-grabbing, Mr get bad, got a spot in the game and bet his last few dollars.

A J's desire to borrow other people's property without permission hadn't changed a bit. For some reason, he was obsessed with taking other people's bicycles, and it didn't matter who it belonged to. So it wasn't surprising that when he saw an abandoned ten-speed lying in front of the store on the corner, his criminal instinct told him to take, break, and roll. He got on it and hit the wind!

Monty and Leon had other ideas about enjoying their escape time from the church, and they did what came naturally. In other words, they followed the smell of weed in front of the store, and put their change together, and got one of the locals to buy them a pint of wine. From then on, it was share and share-alike. They passed their wine, and the local boys passed their weed. They got their swerve on, and it didn't take long for them to wind up looking slack-eyed, silly, and talking shit.

Well, to sum up, this little adventure, Popsicle wound up losing most of his money in the crap game he was in, which resulted in him getting pissed off and talking shit. D.A showboated in the basketball game he was in and pissed the other team off by hustling them out of their money. A.J. jacked a bicycle and went on a sightseeing trip all over the city. And Monty and Leon got so high on wine and pot that they couldn't tell the difference between shit and shoe polish. But, it was time for the five wise guy's adventure to end because reality was about to set in.

It turned out that shit in the neighborhood was getting thick; a lot of attitudes were changing. To The level of unrest from the residents on this urban plantation was soaring to a new height.

Two Cincinnati cop cars pulled up and stopped at the corner of Race and 13th street. They had gotten a complaint about a stolen ten-speed bicycle. The mother of the boy whose bike was missing had called and was giving them a description of the stolen bike. However, there were no witnesses to identify the thief who took it. But it didn't take long for someone who knew A.J. to spot him riding it through the city. As a matter of fact, the boy that knew him happened to be a cousin to the boy whose bike was stolen. But the bad part of this situation was that the boy was a member of a notorious gang called the Tot-Lot-Posses.

Nevertheless, during this time, once again, turmoil was on the rise at the church. It seems that there were different points of view about the Bible scripture regarding the Prophet Abraham. Some of the girls contested the fact that Joseph was born through the bloodline of Isaac. Kim, Angie, and Tamara were all arguing that he was, and they were getting fed up with the idiotic way of thinking the other girls had.

As a result, one stupid comment led to another, until finally, these girls set-it-off. They stood face to face in a shouting match arguing their point, and when no neutral ground could be gained, they started hurling insults at each other:

(Marlene) "Kim, you're stupid, your mama must have dropped you on your head when you were born. You don't know what you're talking about."

(Kim) "Wait a minute, Heifer! You're the one whose stupid, and your mama had to slap the ugly off you when you were born just to get your own dog to play with you."

(Marlene) "Girl-friend, your mama's a alcoholic, and she drinks so much that she put your corner liquor store out of business."

(Kim) "Your mama's so Butch that a talent scout got her a job playing fullback for the hefty Ho's!"

(Marlene) "Wait a minute, Bitch! Don't be talking about my mama!

(Kim) "Okay, I'll talk about your daddy then. Your daddy is so tight with money that his ass squeaks when he walks. You didn't get your first pair of shoes until you were 11 years old.

(Marlene) "Awe girl, Your daddy is so damn ugly, it looks like he got shot in the face with a Shit-Gun."

(Kim) "Heifer, your faggot ass daddy sucks dicks longer than a flashlight shining through the back end of a school bus."

"You Fat Nasty Heifer!"

"You Black Scum Bag Bitch!"

Well, in the split second that followed, Marlene caught Kim by surprise with a swing that barely missed hitting her in the face. Kim faded back to miss the swing and quickly came back with a punch that hit Marlene square in the jaw. Marlene lost her balance, back peddled, and flipped into the row of pews behind her. Then, with Marlene out of commission, her sister, Mary, stepped in to retaliate. She grabbed Kim by the hair and pulled off a wig. So, she flung it in the air and charged Kim like a mad bull.

But Angie was quick to stick out her foot and trip her when she charged. When she fell to the floor, Angie jumped on her back, grabbed a Bible from the pew, and started beating her in the back of her head with it. After that, Tamara wound up squaring off with the oldest sister, Marsha. They went to knuckle city–looking like welter-weight boxers. They sparred for a while, then they locked heads and fell to the floor– rocking and rolling in the middle of the church aisle. But it finally came to an end when Alvin and a couple of the Deacons broke them up.

Grandma Ella didn't know what to do about these girls. She had just been through the same kind of drama with the other girls, and she was getting frustrated with the lot of them. But for some reason, she didn't let it bother her. Instead, she took this as a sign to pray about it right then and there.

Meanwhile, police officers took a walk through Washington Park to ask questions about the bicycle theft. They went to the corner stores and randomly checked i.d.s. But when the cops finally got to Monty and Leon, they were higher than two kites in a windstorm.

"Hey, Shit for brains, come here--you to scum bag! Did either one of you boys see anybody riding around on a new ten-speed bicycle this morning?" Monty said, "No sir, officer, sir. I swear to God! Shit, I thought I was blind till I seent you walk up here! Ain't that right, Leon." "Yeah, That's Right, we blind, we ain't seent Shit!!"

Well, the cops couldn't do anything but look at them like they were a couple of fools and tell them to get the hell away from there; anything else would have been a waste of time. And thank God they were smart enough to disappear through the next alley they saw and head back to the church.

As for D. A., he felt the hatred building up in the teams he and his crew were beating, and he decided to cut his game short because of the jealousy that was brewing. He and his two-man crew had already won five out of five games—at five dollars a game, and some of the downtown street-ballers were pissed off because they couldn't stop him from scoring, so, in turn, they got mad and started fouling him.

But he had already gotten what he came for, and when he saw the police asking Monty and Leon questions, he got wise and decided to shake and break back to the church too. And a few minutes later he caught up with Monty and Leon.

And as for Popsicle, his luck had run out, and he was down to his last dollar. So, when he saw the cops patrolling the streets, he saw a natural opportunity come into view, and he was bold enough to do it. He had been in this same situation at least a dozen times before. Therefore, he went into his bag of tricks and used the element of misdirection to pull off his caper.

On his turn to throw the dice, he recklessly overthrew them to the far side of the alley, and while everybody was looking for the dice, he stood up and shouted: "Here Comes Five-0! Here Comes Five -0!" And the split second that everyone looked up the alley in the same direction wChapter Four

Road Tripping

The Mission Begins

Grandma Williams and Grandma Walker were themes of the same variation. In the past, the more crap a child got away with was equally proportionate to the punishment they'd receive—if not more. They both believed in family values and old school discipline.

Anyway, it was time to go. Samantha looked up at her Grandmother with sad eyes and said, "I'm going to miss you Grandma." David spoke his heart as well. "I'm going to miss you too Grandma." Then they both put their arms around her and held her tight. Grandma welled up inside, and her voice was filled with sadness when she said. "I'm going to miss you babies too."

Then Samantha backed away, and sobbing and trembling with fear; she said, "I love you Grandma." Grandma said, "I love you too Samantha." Then, she ran to her Grandma again, wrapped her arms around her waist, and held on to her tight. So, Grandma held her head to her bosom, stroked her hair, and soothed away her fear. "Come on now, she said. We'll be back together soon. The time will just fly by. You and David will have so much fun that you won't even miss me, and I'll call you in a few days to see how you're doing, O'K, I promise."

After hearing that, Samantha was relieved. She wiped the tears from her face and gave her Grandma a big smile. Then she said, O'K, Grandma, I'll be waiting for you to call. Then Grandma stood at the front door and watched them walk to the bus. As David was getting on the bus, she noticed he was wearing that same pair of raggedy gym-shoes, but it was too late to stop him– he was already on the bus. He slapped Alvin a high-five and immediately ran to the back of the bus to sit with A.J. Nevertheless, Alvin stepped off the bus and spoke to her. "Hi, Aunt Jan," and she responded, "High, Alvin. Hey Alvin, will you make sure that boy puts on his good pair of shoes before he gets to church? "No problem, Auntie, I will." "You all have a good time, and be careful driving, Alvin."

Well, as soon as Samantha got on the bus, she found the nerve to square off with Alvin. She got to the top step two feet in front of his face and said, "you heard my Grandma! You better drive this bus like you got some sense, and Don't be Speeding!" But coming from a family with five sisters, Alvin refused to be intimidated. So, he eased back in his seat, looked her up and down, and told her to go sit her little Peter Pan ass down so he could drive the bus. Then, he started the bus and mumbled some profound words. Samantha heard him say: (I'm on a mission from God!). An exasperating, "Oh Boy," came from her mouth, along with a look at him like he was a nut. Then she strolled down the aisle to the back of the bus.

Although this was the first time David met A.J., they took to each other like fish to the water. Within minutes of talking, A.J. had dubbed David with the alias D.A. due to his middle name (Alafia). Earlene, Tamara, and Danielle were all sitting in the middle seats. They were gabbing on and on about all the things they were going to do this summer. But when Samantha reached them, she was timid and shy. She was the youngest member of the bunch; however, they all took the time to welcome her with open arms to ease her.

Meanwhile, as they all prepared to get comfortable, they looked toward the front and saw Alvin pop a tape in his cassette player. Then he stuck a pair of earbuds in his ears and put on his sunglasses. That's when the first thought crossed their mind that they better get ready for the wildest bus ride of their lives.

Grandma Williams was still at the front door with a bewildered look on her face. She was trying to figure out where she saw that raggedy-ass bus before. Then it came to her—it was the same broken down jitney that was in the empty lot next to her sister's house.

She busted out laughing and started talking to herself. (lord, somebody must have been doing a whole lot of praying, she thought. Because whatever they did to get that thing up and running was short of a miracle).

Anyway, Alvin had been a metro-city bus driver for twenty years and knew all the city streets, back-alleys, shortcuts, and where all the main potholes were like he knew the back of his hand. But he still had one vice—listening to James Brown while he was driving. He'd put on his music to drown out everything and everybody around him, and listening to James Brown was the stimulus that aroused his soul and allowed him to "Get on the Good-Foot," and likewise, it triggered his reckless style of driving.

The task ahead for Alvin was a big one. He had to make several more stops until he picked up everyone on his list. That meant traveling from one neighborhood to another all around the city.

Therefore, after he buckled his seat belt, put on his sunglasses, and popped a James Brown tape in his cassette player, he "Got on the Good foot. He popped the clutch and took off like he was coming out of a pit-stop at the Indy-500. He drove up the street and down to the bottom of Sheffield Road in a matter of seconds.

When he reached the bottom, there was a 25mph speed limit sign, so he came to a complete stop to observe the landscape. There was a long winding road with fenced-in pastureland on both sides of the road ahead of him. The reason for the fence was that there might be a few dozen heads of cattle grazing at any given time. Now and then, the cattle would get spooked by the sound of loud cars and trucks passing by and go astray—at times trampling over the fence and winding up on the road. Furthermore, on this particular morning, there was a thick fog hovering over the road ahead.

A little way down the road, he spotted a cow in the middle of the fog-filled road, then another and another. And despite these kids' fear, protesting, and hollering at him to not do what he was obviously going to do, it was useless. They realized that he had those earbuds stuck in his ear. He couldn't hear a word they were saying. He was tuned in and turned on to James Brown so much that nothing else mattered.

Regardless of the situation, Alvin perused the road ahead, and sure enough, he took off like a kamikaze pilot on a search - destroy mission.

He turned on his bright lights, blew his horn, and with his mind being absorbed with the thought of completing the mission he set out to do, he continued driving with reckless abandon.

These kids had no other recourse except to respond in unison with a long, drawn-out: AWE … … … … … … … … SHIT!

He zig-zagged his way through a milelong stretch of cows and cow manure in less than 10 seconds. He swerved left in front of the first cow and grazed its jaw, making it turn around and go back to the field that it came from. He broke to the right of the second cow and ran over a huge pile of cow manure. All of a sudden, the rear end of the bus fishtailed one-way, then the other, and it just so happened that the back end of the bus smacked a cow on its rear end and pushed it across the road into the field on the other side of the road.

Several yards later, he saw two more cows crossing the road. One was behind the other with about three yards between them, and he immediately mashed on the accelerator and shot right between them like he was in a demolition derby. The two cows scampered away in different directions only to wind up, falling over in the ditches on the sides of the road.

Then he got to a bend in the road and couldn't see around the corner. A cow was standing in the middle of the road. It was mooing and seemed to be mesmerized by the bus engine's sound and the oncoming light in the street. Alvin slowed down a little, but he was still traveling a little too fast when he saw the cow standing there. He quickly hit the breaks to avoid hitting it, but by now, his front and back tires were covered with cow manure, and the bus skidded several feet before Alvin could get control of it, and as a result, the bus went into a 360 degree flat spin. Bodies pummeled and tumbled from one side of the bus to the other;

they spent completely around in a circle in the middle of the road before they came to a stop.

Anyway, after they stopped spinning, Alvin got his bearings together and made a U-Turn. He drove off the road into the grass. Then he drove right past the cow that was miraculously still standing in the same spot and got back on the road.

Well, when they finally reached the end of the road, there was a sigh of relief. The Holy Crusaders had made it this far, but there were a few more stops to make before they reached the church. Consequently, all of them were seriously wondering if they would make it there before they met their maker.

They were at the intersection of the main road, where they made a right turn and rode a half-mile to the first light. Then, they made a left turn onto Route 42 and followed it down a hill—up a hill—and down another hill until they reached the I-75 entrance ramp and merged into the highway traffic. Not more than three minutes later, he got off at the Lincoln Heights exit and went straight to big mama's house, where three more cousins were waiting: Leroy, Sparkle, and Leon.

Leon alone was a nerve-racking nuisance. And their mother had to deal with daily problems that involved keeping him from staying high on pot all day, keeping Leroy out of jail from selling crack, and keeping Sparkle away from a hot-tail group of girls who would do any and everything to get money. Other than that, keeping a steady job and enough food in the house was a day to day concern.

Anyway, after he picked them up, he drove to the upper sub to pick up cousins Lee, his sister, Lavada, and Alvin's favorite cousin,

Little Gary—AKA-Popsicle. But first, he took a short ride through the hood to see how much things had changed, and where he encountered several amusing situations.

The first sight was a group of angry people shouting and cursing at the police. They called them a bunch of no good ass crooks on the take. Alvin heard some of the conversations and kept on driving, saying that some shit never changes. In most cases, the cops would harass the dope boys, take their drugs, take their money, locked them up, and let them out the next morning. That was standard procedure and the modus operandi of the LHPD. Most of the time, the police had more drugs to get high on and sold more drugs than the local dope boys.

As he drove further up the street, and before he could turn the corner, he almost ran into an old wino who walked out in the middle of the road. He forced Alvin to make a sudden stop. And after he stopped, the man banged on the hood of the bus and shouted, "What's my name, God-dammit." He stood there mumbling with his body weaving back and forth, saying the same thing over and over. Then he stared inside the bus with a frightful look on his face. But Alvin knew the from a long time ago, so he got off the bus and helped the man to the curb where he sat him down. Then Alvin reached in his pocket and handed the man a few dollars. He used to be a brilliant architect and a brick mason back in his day. He had built nursing homes and houses throughout the city, but for some reason, he lost his mind, and he set fires to the places he would build before he even finished them.

Anyway, after that, he drove midways down the hill to the Valley Homes–the projects where Popsicle lived. And as soon as they turned the corner, they saw the cherry-lipped bandit. Alvin spotted him in the parking lot shaking a pair of dice. He got the nickname Popsicle because when he was younger, his mother spoiled him rotten. Whenever she took him to the corner store, he would beg, cry, whine, and demand that she buy him a Popsicle. And if she didn't, he'd pitch a bitch-fit. He'd lay down in the middle of the floor kicking and crying until she or someone did—sometimes even strangers would buy him a popsicle to shut him up.

Anyway, Alvin pulled in the parking lot and saw him in a crap game with five older boys. He was in the middle, down on one knee with his hand raised in the air shaking a pair of dice, swearing to send all of them home broke. So, he threw the dice, and when they landed, his heart sunk. "Snake eyes, sorry little nigga, you lose!" the boys laughed and teased him relentlessly. They told him to: "take your young, broke black-ass home, and don't go away mad, just go the fuck away—you little bastard!"

Popsicle was pissed, in more ways than one. He had just lost all his money, and the lesson in humility that came from those boys sure as hell didn't help his self-esteem.

Well, as it turned out, there couldn't have been a better time for Popsicle to pull off what he did next. Popsicle went into a tirade and started cussing and fussing at everybody around him. He went wild– jumping up and down on top of the money and kicking it all around. They all thought he had lost his mind. But his next move was unbelievable. All of a sudden, he fell on top of the money, but when he got up, he had a hand full of bills, and he stampeded his way through those older boys like a Heisman Trophy winner.

Alvin had just turned the bus around and was headed back out the parking lot when he saw Popsicle kicking up rocks running away from that mob of thugs. Suddenly, one of the boys caught up with him and grabbed him by the collar of his shirt and held on, but Popsicle changed gears on the boy and came straight out of that shirt. In that same moment, Alvin opened the door to the bus, and Popsicle dove through the bus doors like he was making an endzone play. And he leaped so far that he wound up laying across Alvin's lap.

Alvin's timing was perfect, but when he pulled the door shut, those boys were still running alongside the bus, banging on the door, trying to pry it open. So, Alvin went to work, putting his years of driving skills to good use. He mashed the gas pedal and made an impossible 45 degree turn out of that parking lot. He was traveling so fast, and the turn was so sharp that the bus tilted on two of its side wheels going around the corner.

Well, they got away, but not before the back of the bus was bombarded by rocks, bottles, and sticks, and anything that they could find to throw at it. And while everyone on the bus was terrified, Popsicle was happy and as relieved as a convict that just made parole; he narrowly escaped another near-death beat-down. That being the case, he ran to the back of the bus and taunted them through the window. They couldn't hear him, but they sure as hell knew what he was saying. "Y'all some Busters, you can't catch me, Y'all some chumps!" Then he did the cabbage patch–pausing now and then in the middle of his dance to blurt out: "You Can't Touch This."

Well, Despite the jeopardizing situation Popsicle put them through, Alvin had one more stop to make in this wacky city, and he knew it would have to be a quick one. He drove back to the upper sub to pick up Big Lee and Lavada in the nick of time, and they were more than ready to go. The next-door neighbors had just called the police because of all the noise; Lee had just blinded his stepdaddy with an ass-whooping. This stout fifteen-year-old boy was tired of seeing his mother with black eyes every time he came home drunk. And he was tired of him terrorizing his baby sister, so his pint up hostility finally came to a boiling point, and he exploded. Therefore, they were ready to go with their bags packed as soon as Alvin drove up.

Alvin fled from the scene just as the police were arriving. He eventually got back on the freeway and headed straight to his sister Lorraine's house. Then got off the highway and stopped at the red light at the intersection. But when he took off again, they heard the sound of something tapping at the back of the bus. Alvin looked through the side-view mirror and saw his bald, melon head nephew on his bicycle in the middle of the street; he was hanging onto the side of the bus.

Monty was up to his dangerous games again, and not only did he get their attention, but he also got the attention of the semi-truck driver in the left lane coming straight towards him. The driver didn't have much time to make a complete stop, so he started blowing his horn from a block away. Suddenly, Alvin decided to speed up and make a right turn instead of going straight. A split second later, Monty grabbed hold of the bus and followed it out of the path of the oncoming truck, but little did he know that his mother almost had a heart attack watching the whole incident from her porch on the next street.

That was a close call for Monty because if Alvin hadn't made that right turn, he would have wound up lying next to a grease spot in the middle of rode. Nevertheless, he was about to reap the benefit of his good luck in exchange for a sore ass when he got home.

When the bus pulled in the yard, Monty was right behind it on his ten-speed. And when Lorraine spotted him, she immediately did a two-handed vault off the front porch railing into the yard and went straight to where he was standing. He laughed and joked with Earlene and A.J. through the bus window when she shocked the shit out of him. She immediately started beating him with the hard rubber house slipper she pulled off her foot.

Monty tried to bob and weave and cover-up from the stinging blows she was hitting him with. She hit him upside his head and all over his body with that slipper, and she was too damn mad and too damn fast with that slipper to let any open area of contact on his body go unpunished.

The kids on the bus started out feeling sorry for him when they saw the merciless beating he was getting. They couldn't help from cringing and squinting their eyes every time they heard the solid sound of those smacks to his body. However, what came out of his mouth next changed all of that.

After what seemed like an eternity, Monty made the mistake of calling her the "B" word. He must have been delirious from the ass whooping she was putting on him and so fed up with all the licks to his head that he shouted: "Stop hitting me bitch!" Well, the fickle finger of fate changed everything because the sympathy they once had for the num nut turned into instructions on how to beat his ass.

A.J. Hollered out the bus window, "Hit him again, Aunt Lorraine, show him what ya working with."

Earlene Hollered, "Yeah, hit that fool again, Aunt Lorraine. Knock the meat off his off his ass! He needs his ass whooped!"

D.A. said: "You need to use a night-stick on his Ass."

Danielle said: "Yeah, knock the taste out of his mouth, Aunt Lorraine. He ain't got no business cussing at you."

Sam and Sparkle got in on the act, and both of them shouted out the window at the same time, "Yeah, Kick his ass."

Leon heard everything they said and couldn't think of a thing to say, so he just said, "Yeah, what they said. Ehee, heeheeheeheehee."

Anyway, right after that devastating beat-down, they gather up what was left of Monty, got him on the bus, and continued the mission. This time, instead of getting on the highway, Alvin took a shortcut. He went straight down Paddock Road, which took him about ten minutes to get to sister Norlene's house. Once there, he would pick up Big Kim, Ernie, and baby sister Angie.

When he pulled up, they were standing at the door—well dressed, ready to go, and looking very sophisticated. So, with Alvin pressed for time, they said their goodbyes and got on the bus without delay.

Well, Alvin had one more stop to make before he could head to the church. That stop was the Greyhound station downtown.

Little Walter–AKA-Chunk was riding the bus up from Atlanta, and hopefully, he'd be there right on time to pick him up. And as such, he was. The bus had just dropped him off.

From there, they traveled West through a downtown portion of the city to Vine Street. They made a right turn and went up Vine to Mulberry—one of the city's steepest hills. It took a while with the bus filled and luggage everywhere, but that yellow, rusty little jitney bus performed like "The little engine that could." It smoked and choked. Stuttered, and puttered and backfired, until it made it to the top of that hill to the church.

as the same split second that he grabbed a fist full of the money off the ground and took off running down the alley in the opposite direction.

It was unbelievable and a wondrous sight to see how fast that boy could run. And when those thugs took off after him, you could tell just from watching that they'd never catch him. Popsicle took off like a runaway slave with a gang of bloodhounds on his ass.

But, when he got to the next street, those thugs were still chasing him, and that's when he went from low gear to high gear, hitting every gear in between. It just so happened that he saw A.J. up ahead riding on that bicycle; he caught up with him, waved at him, and ran right past him.

When A.J. heard the footsteps behind him, he looked back to see and hear all the fussing and cussing from that gang of thugs and figured out that they were after Popsicle. But Popsicle had put so much distance between them that they just gave up.

After they gave up, A.J. quickly sped up to catch up with Popsicle, and as soon as he did, one of the gang members from the

Tot-Lot-Posse spotted him and pointed him out as the thief that stole his cousin's bike.

Anyway, a few ticks later, they all met up at the bottom corner of the intersection. A.J., D. A., Monty, Leon, and Popsicle were all there with two blocks and a steep hill to tackle before they reached the church.

But suddenly, from a distance, they heard the sound of angry voices coming from the playground on the next corner. They turned to look and saw one of the boys pointing his finger at them, saying: "There's the motherfucker that stole my cousin's bike!" Another guy asked: "Who are those niggas?" And another one said, "They ain't from around here." Well, with that being said they all recited the gang slogan out loud: "Pins and needles, needles and pins: a dead nigga is a nigga that don't grin!"

After that, twenty gang members were walking toward them fast, fast, fast. By the time they figured out what was going on, A.J. took off across the street and headed up the hill. But, one of the gang members spotted him and fired his pistol at him. And when Monty, D.A., Leon, and Pop heard the shots, they stormed up that hill like soldiers on a beachfront–scared to death.

Soon afterward, a miraculous event occurred. A.J. made it to the second block and was at the corner about to turn up the hill when he saw an aberration standing there. It stood over seven feet tall with a Hood covering its face, and it was holding a thick wooden staff.

When he got closer, the aberration banged the staff on the ground. It sounded like thunder, and it shook the ground so hard that that bicycle stood straight up on its back wheel– A.J. fell off and hit the ground. He couldn't believe what had just happened, but he didn't have time to think about it either—he looked back, then forward, and kept on running as fast as he could up that hill to the church.

When the rest of the boys reached the corner, they saw the seven-foot, hooded aberration on the corner as well, but their attention span and their ears were more in tune with the sound of the footsteps they heard behind them and the sound of the bullets whizzing over their heads.

Likewise, they turned the corner and ran up that hill right behind A.J. But all of a sudden; they heard that thunderous bang again. Even more miraculous was when that aberration stood out on the sidewalk, opened its arms, and from out of nowhere, a strong gust of wind came and blew those gang members and the bicycle back down the hill and across the intersection.

When they made it to the church, they opened the doors and ran inside, huffing and puffing; they were out of breath and relieved to still be alive.

Anyway, they were right on time for the Sunday Service, and everyone was in the process of convening upstairs for the sermon.

And instead of viewing these boys as missing in action, their sudden, timely presence was looked at as their eagerness to hear a lesson about the Lord.

CHAPTER SIX

HOLY HYPNOSIS

While the congregation settled in their seats, Reverend Kimble approached the pulpit to announce the day's sermon topic. After that, the church entertained them with a selection while taking up another collection for the church. Sister Althea played the organ while the choir backed up an out of town guest who sang a popular gospel song.

> Master, the tempest is raging.
> The billows are tossing high.
> The sky is o'er shadowed with
> Blackness
> No shelter or help is nigh.
> Carest Thou not that we perish?
> How canst Thou lie asleep
> When each moment so madly
> is threatening
> A grave in the angry deep
> The winds and the waves shall

obey my will; peace be still.
Whether the wrath of the
storm-tossed sea
Or demons or men or
whatever it be
No water can swallow the ship
where lies
The Master of ocean and earth
and skies
They shall sweetly obey my will
Peace be still, peace be still
They all shall sweetly obey my
will, peace be still, peace be still.
When you're burdened: Peace
When you're lonely: Peace
When you're hungry: Peace

Following the end of the song, the church congregation showed their appreciation with the overwhelming sound of applauds. And after the sound of their applauds had died down, Reverend Kimble returned to the pulpit. However, as soon as he opened his mouth to speak, he was silenced by the loud sound of thunder that echoed through the church.

And as such, the entire church congregation looked to the back of the church and then front to the pulpit to see where the noise came from. Then a blinding light swept through the church that lasted all but a split second. Was this real, or were they hallucinating, they thought to themselves. But when their vision cleared, and they regained their sight, they saw an enormously tall figure of someone or something standing at the pulpit next to Reverend Kimble. Whoever it was, wore a long, black and gold hooded cloak, and it wielded a long, thick, black wooden staff.

After it removed its hood, the gasping sound of fear from disbelief filled the room. They recognized that it was a woman, but she resembled the likes of a mythological creature from the past. She had bird-like facial features that glistened like a piece of shiny black coal. Her eyes were dark and piercing like an eagle's, and she had a white ivory necklace around her neck. But even more chilling was the sound of her deep-dry gravelly voice when she spoke.

"JAMBO, WATU WASURI—GREETINGS, BEAUTIFUL
    PEOPLE
I HAVE BEEN WATCHING YOU.
I AM THE JAMAICAN PRIESTESS MAMA CREOLARD.
I HAVE BEEN SENT FROM THE AFTER WORLD TO BRING
    YOU A MESSAGE OF LIFE.
PROTECT YOUR CHILDREN.
PROTECT YOUR CHILDREN FROM THE (SEEDS OF
    TEMPTATION). PROTECT YOUR CHILDREN'S
    CHILDREN
SO THAT THEY MAY MULTIPLE IN BEAUTY,
AND MULTIPLY THE BEAUTY OF THE EARTH.
LIFE IS A PRECIOUS STEPINGSTONE.
USE IT TO ATTAIN A GLORIOUS DEATH.
THERE IS EVERLASTING LIFE IN THE AFTER WORLD.
AS IT HAS BEEN ORDAINED BY JAH ON THIS EARTH,
IT IS JAH'S WILL THAT IT TO BE DONE."
"NOW, BEAUTIFUL PEOPLE OF JAH,
DANCE TO THE RHYTHM OF THE DRUMS

AND CELEBRATE LIFE WITH ME,

AND MY RETURN TO THE AFTER WORLD".

With that being said, the sound of Congo drums commenced playing a slow rhythmic beat. Mama Creolard's dark piercing eyes scoured the room like they were in search of prey. They haunted and intimidated everyone in the church, especially the likes of A.J.—who, with an open bible covering his face, sunk down deeper and deeper into the pew.

Nevertheless, in a matter of seconds, the drummer started beating his bass drum so loud that everyone could feel it. The bass guitar player started plucking his bass so hard and loud that the church windows vibrated. And Sister Althea seemed to be possessed on the organ, screeching out sounds and notes so funky that they could've made the dead get up and dance. There was, without a doubt a supernatural spirit in the church because soon afterwards, a feeling of euphoria and bliss overcame everyone inside.

Hands were clapping, feet were tapping, and tambourines were wrapping. Great big women jumped up on the floor as if they had been reborn. They put their hands on their hip and danced in a circle from right to left; then they put a hand on their hip and danced from left to right—including Mrs. Walker.

The spirit even hit deep inside the girls. Kim, Tamara, and Angie couldn't contain themselves any longer. They danced, shouted praises, and started speaking in tongues while falling to the floor, going into convulsions, and squirming around in the church aisles.

Suddenly, Mama Creolard exerted a loud, frightful, supernatural squawking that sounded like an enormous bird. Then she stretched her arms out wide and brought her staff down to the floor and banged it three times. A powerful gust of wind blew through the church; the windows slammed shut, the doors locked uptight, and the sunlight shining through the stain-glass windows of the church got brighter and brighter. The flickering light from one window to the next made the inside of the church look like a kaleidoscope.

Immediately following this hallowed experience, little children and babies in their strollers began speaking in tongue. The Holy Water under the pulpit turned blue and bubbled out of its container, and all nine collection plates were miraculously filled up with money.

Then, the sound of the Congo drums started beating faster, harder, and louder; it was as if they were in the deepest, darkest part of the African jungle. The drummer, the bass player, and the organist were mesmerized by the conga drums' beat, and their souls became a part of the music.

The unearthly spirit possessed the choir. They began to sway back and forth and round-about in circular motions. Even the sound of wild animals was present–giving the church an African safari like ambiance. Then the church members witnessed the seven-foot-tall Jamaican Priestess do her bird dance, and as such, they fell under the spell of her hypnotic power and began dancing like they were in a Voodoo Ritual.

They danced, danced, and danced with no recollection of time or what was happening to them. Then, several hours later, as sudden and miraculously as Mama Creolard appeared, she mysteriously disappeared. After that, there was complete silence in the church. But the entire church congregation, with over 300 people in attendance, were still in a semi-hypnotic trance after Mama Creolard left. And not one of them could acknowledge or deny her presence in the church. But that didn't last long. A.J. inadvertently broke the silence when he slowly slid up from his seat with his bible wide-open covering his face.

And when he got the courage to bring the bible down from over his face, he stood up, looked around the room, and a split second later, with no regard for where he was, he blurted out loud: "Whew! I'm Glad That Bitch Is Gone!"

Mrs. Walker abruptly turned around in her seat and frowned at him with a look of disgust on her face. She was too far away to slap him in the throat with a backhand. But Earlene knew what to do; she hauled off and slapped him in the back of his peanut-shaped head. Well, Leon was sitting right next to A.J. When he saw her slap him, and it just tore him to pieces; he couldn't stop laughing: "Ehee, heehee heeheeheeheeheehee, Ehee, heeheeheeheeheehee, Ehee, heeheeheehee, Ehee, eeheeheeheeheehee!"

But the strange thing was that, when the church members heard the silly sound of his laughter, it caught on like an infectious disease. And soon afterward, more than half the people in the church were laughing at the sound of his laughter.

As for The Reverend Kimble, when he came out of his zombie-like trance, he saw all the money piled up in those collection plates and was thrilled beyond words; it was like a dream come true; moreover, his last announcement was that church was over.

When they stepped outside and saw the sun setting, it was eight o'clock in the evening. They couldn't believe how fast time went by. Nevertheless, the overall mindset that these rambunctious cousins had was still intact. They didn't let the notion of a supernatural act happening in the church affect them in the slightest way.

CHAPTER SEVEN

HOME COMING/AUNT ELLA'S HOUSE

After these half-starved kids piled on the bus, Mrs. Walker had Alvin stop at the closest KFC to get a two-piece chicken meal for everyone. Fortunately, it was a quick trip because it was only a half-mile down the road. And as quick as they got there, they devoured their two-piece meal even quicker.

Ten minutes later, Alvin pulled off the main road coming from town onto the freeway. After several minutes on the freeway, he pulled off at the Hopple Street exit and made a left turn at the intersection. After diving a mile through a business district, he reached a side street and took a small stretch of road to the end of Colerain Ave. Then he drove down a back alley and pulled into an empty lot next to the house.

Most of the kids had never been there before; it was their first time. Nevertheless, it was dark outside, and not easy to see how it looked from the outside. It was a tall, spooky-looking three-story row house. A few of the gray panels of siding were missing from the top portion of the house, but for the most part, it was a spacious and comfortable place to live and raise a family

Anyway, as soon as Alvin parked the bus, everyone grabbed their belongings and pushed their way to the front of the bus. Although there were no lights on the inside of the house, outside in the yard, there was just enough light for them to see the gate in the middle of the fence that surrounded the house.

Is just so happened that the light that let them see as much as they did see came from under the hood of a car on the side of the house. Uncle Riley—Aunt Ella's Husband, was still under the hood working on it; he had been there since early that morning, and he was determined to get it running. He was obviously frustrated because he was mumbling and fidgeting with his tools, trying to find the right size to replace a part.

Anyway, as soon as they got off the bus, they heard barking and scuffling feet going back and forth. It was Rah-Mel, a full-grown German Shepherd, and he was Uncle Riley's pride and joy. His ferocious bark sent chills up and down their backs. Lucky for them, he was inside a five by ten foot caged fence inside the confines of the fence in the backyard.

Aunt Ella didn't take any mess off him or the last two mutts Riley brought home. If she got tired of hearing him barking, she'd stare him dead in his eyes with a look that could make the second-hand on a clock stop. Then she'd tell him to Shut up and Go Sit down! It worked every time. Rah-Mel would walk away with his tail between his legs and lay down in his cage.

Anyway, Rah-Mel could smell the food they'd been eating when they passed by his cage, and it sent him into a wild frenzy.

And as such, being scared out of their wits, these kids cautiously passed by his cage and ran up the porch steps—pushing their way inside the backdoor.

Meanwhile, lurking in the darkness, Alvin and A J. were the last ones to leave the bus. Alvin had good reason to be last. He didn't want to be noticed by his daddy. He knew that if he saw him, he was going to ask him for help fixing that car, and Alvin had no intentions of getting dirty and greasy and being up all night.

Nevertheless, Mrs. Walker had already stopped to give Riley a chicken dinner on the way to the house, and through their exchange of information, he knew that Alvin was somewhere close by.

Sure enough, the next sound heard was his daddy's voice saying: hey boy, come here and help me put this engine in this car." Alvin was pissed when he heard that! He was tired, sleepy, and hungry, just like everybody else. Anyone listening could tell that he was overflowing with disgust because he began mumbling to himself: "God-dam, daddy! I don't feel like fooling with that raggedy-ass car tonight! Shit! Hell Naw!" His daddy didn't hear him, but A. J.'s ears were wide open, and he could tell just how upset his dad was, but that didn't stop him from snickering. Then he saw him walk away and disappear down an alley. And knowing that his grandfather would never ask him for help, A. J. offered to help him anyway, not meaning it, but he told him: "I'll help you, Grandpa."

The Next Morning

Well, the next morning, Aunt Ella was up early preparing breakfast for the kids. She was in the kitchen, stirring a huge pot of oatmeal. The only early risers to assist her were Lavada and Danielle. They sat up the kitchen table with the necessary amount of bowls, cups, and spoons.

Anyway, when the oatmeal was done, they sat down at the table to eat before the others made their random descent to the kitchen.

The first one down the steps was Samantha. It took a while, but the eight-year-old, feisty filly made it down that long, narrow flight of steps from the third floor with no problem. She and the girls were up late last night talking and getting to know each other. They talked and talked and talked and realized that they had a lot in common.

For instance, all of them were so stingy with their money. They could squeeze the eagle on a dollar bill until it screamed. And they all used the same methods of operation against their brothers: blackmail, extortion, and snitching. And although they appeared to be shy, sweet, and gentle angels, they could also be as mean as a mongoose.

The next two occupants to appear were Kim and Tamara. They were the oldest females of the bunch. They were also up late last night recalling old friends and old times. They were bright, intelligent girls with gifted voices, and they loved listening to and singing gospel songs and preaching the word. But, if you pushed them too far, they'd "Tap Dance on Some Ass."

Whistling, He-hawing, and humming their way down the steps next was Alvin Junior and Walter Junior; (AKA) A. J. and Chunky, respectively. They had a long night of reminiscing, fun, and laughter. They talked about things in the past and played video games until they fell asleep. They were like brothers growing up. For A.J., it was like losing his best friend when his Aunt Wanda packed them up and moved to Atlanta. Nevertheless, A.J. still got to see Chunk every other summer. They were two care-free, happy-go-lucky kids in the pursuit of happiness–which included each, every, and any kind of prank imaginable.

Squeaking down the stair steps next, in their size 15 shoes, was Big Lee and David Alafia, (AKA) D.A. Their dads are brothers, and as such, they had a close bond. They were very athletically endowed, and they loved sports, mainly football, and basketball, and on any given day, they'd hustle for money playing basketball or betting on football games.

The next two to the breakfast table were Earlene and Angie. Last night they got to know each other all over again. They talked about everything from boys and school, to life in general. Earlene always had Angie's back if anything went wrong with her. And Angie had her back. She'd calm Earlene down when she got upset or if she did anything to get in herself trouble.

Bringing up the rear were two legends in their mind, Ernie and Monty. They eased on down the stairs to the breakfast table, rapping to a Hip-Hop tune. These dudes were self-absorbed. Ernie thought he was a Mack, and Monty thought he was a gangster rapper. Nonetheless, they were just two aspiring lovers and rappers with delusions of grandeur.

Anyway, the last loafers down the steps were the "Scum off the Pond." If any of these kids needed religion, it was these three, Little Gary-AKA(Popsicle), little Leon, and Leroy. They were the undisputed products of their environment. Popsicle could be described as a rambling, scamming, gambling, money thief. He kept a 7-inch switchblade in his back pocket, and his extracurricular activities included: shooting craps, purse snatching, carjacking, rolling winos in alleys, and stealing the stink out of shit!

Leroy was just as scandalous. He was a pistol-packing bad-ass and in the developmental stage of being a big-time dope-dealing-dumbass. His mom was desperate to get him away from the dope-slinging hustle in the streets and the elements of danger that living in that kind of environment could bring.

Little Leon was another story, He loved getting high, and he did it at every turn— morning, noon, and especially at night. He was always laughing, sounding like a hyena day and day night. And from the sound of his laughter, you'd swear that he was either high as a kite or nut case.

Anyway, these three were the last ones to the kitchen to eat breakfast. But, before they could sit down at the table, the "HNIC'S" Head Negros in Charge—Kim and Tamara, told them to wash their face and hands. And naturally, the reaction that followed was the moans and groans of resentment mumbled under their breath.

CHAPTER EIGHT

THE OATMEAL WAR

Well, everyone sat down at the table to eat, except for Aunt Ella and the other girls, who had eaten earlier, and who was now in the basement washing clothes and putting cups of Kool-Aid in the deep freezer to make ice-balls. Nevertheless, everyone else was there. And as such, A.J. found the perfect opportunity to test out a joke on his new audience. So, he started telling a story about:

The Dog That Could Walk On Water

"Two old men ran into each other at a lake one day with nothing to do but enjoy the peace. One man brought his dog, Fido, with him to keep him company. They sat down and spoke to each other, and then the man with the dog started bragging about his dog, and he told the other man that his dog could do an amazing trick. So, the other man said: "O', Yeah! What can he do?" He said, watch this. He picked up a stick and threw it a little-ways out in the water and told Fido to fetch. The dog walked out on the water, picked the stick up, brought it back, and laid it down next to his master's feet.

He looked at the man and asked him, "Did you notice anything unusual about my dog?" And the man said: "No, I didn't notice anything unusual about your dog." So, he did it again. He threw the stick in the water a little further this time and told Fido to fetch. So, Fido walked out on the water again, picked the stick up, and brought it back to his master.

He turned to look at the man again and said: "Did you notice anything unusual about my dog this time"? And the man said No again.

So, the man was getting frustrated now, and he told him to watch closely. This time he threw the stick halfway across the lake, and he said Fido fetch. Fido ran out across the lake and picked the stick up, then he ran right back with it and gave it to his master. The man looked at him again and said: "Did you notice anything unusual about my dog this time"! The man looked at him and said: "Yeah, Man! That damn dog can't swim"! "Ah ha-ha-ha-ha-ha-ha-ha! Ah, Ha ha ha ha ha ha ha ha ha! You get it! That damn dog can't swim!"

As expected, Leon busted a gut laughing at the joke. But, disgusted by both the joke and A. .J. was Earlene, and what she did next proved how much she disliked his joke, and it was the catalyst that sparked a chain reaction of unbelievable chaos.

First of all, Leon couldn't stop laughing, and he started choking off the oatmeal he was swallowing at the time. However, no-one else at the table seemed to care or give A.J. the time of day. That is until Earlene flung a tablespoon of oatmeal between his eyes

94

and called him a moron. Well, Leon saw that too, and he laughed even louder, and this time, everybody did. But, with a big wad of oatmeal sliding down his nose and dripping from his upper lip–A.J. Retaliated. He slung a lump of oatmeal back at her, but he missed. Earlene ducked, and instead of hitting her, it hit Angie upside her head and knocked her glasses halfway off her face.

"Oh no you didn't negro," She shouted indignantly. Then she immediately flung a huge load of oatmeal right back at him, but her aim was off too, and she wound up plastering Chunk dead in his mouth.

"Dang Angie! He garbled with a load of oatmeal stuck in his mouth. Why did you hit me?" "Oh, I'm sorry, Chunk, I was trying to hit that fool next to you, but my spoon slipped."

After that, the big sisters, Kim and Tamara, got a piece of the action. They were sick and tired of hearing Leon laughing like a nut, and they were tired of hearing Popsicle trying to go for bad selling wolf-tickets. He kept on saying, "I bet nobody better not hit me with that shit!" So, they decided to shut both of them up.

Well, these two must have been thinking the same thought. Because both of them glanced over and saw a twenty-pound bag of rock salt sitting next to the kitchen door–half opened and easy to get to, and a devilish thought popped into these two angles. They looked at the salt and looked at each other and started grinning like two Cheshire cats.

They both grabbed a hand full of the rock salt and mixed it in with the rest of the oatmeal in their bowls. Kim mixed hers up to the size of a baseball and was the first to stand up and rifle it from across the room like a major league pitcher. She hit Popsicle right upside his head, and he went down like a fallen soldier.

Tamara fired away next; her aim was just as good, but instead of hitting Leon in his big ass mouth, she hit him dead in his throat. Not only did she stop him from laughing, the impact from the blow temporarily cut off his breathing.

Anyway, when A.J. saw what happened, he busted a gut laughing. But when Angie saw it she was still seated at the table wiping oatmeal from her hair, and cleaning her, glasses—and of course, mad as hell. So, she sat there in silence and watched her stupid acting cousin, A.J., and the rest of the wild bunch have their fun.

Well, Popsicle had just gotten off the floor, and he was trying to figure out what happened to him. He shouted: "Who hit me, God-dammit!" And Kim spoke up quick, loud, and proud and said: "I did fool, what you going to do about it?" So, he started walking towards her like Mr. Get-Bad– like he was going to do something to her. But when he got close enough to see her holding that cast-iron skillet behind her back, he quickly slowed his roll; he turned around, sat down, and he shut the fuck up. Well, A.J. was tickled when he saw that happen, and he amusingly encouraged Popsicle to stand his ground: He told him: "Go ahead, man— show her what you working with, Popsicle! She's a heavy weight, but don't let that scare you. Do her like Ike did Tina …!"

Angie was still sitting across the table from A.J., and by now, she had wiped all the oatmeal from her hair and cleaned up her glasses. But anyway, she didn't want to have anything else to do with the fight, so she kept her eye on everything going on around her. Everybody had their own private little oat war going on.

After that, A.J. got even sillier. When she put her glasses back on, and A.J saw how thick the lens was, and he just had to say something dumb to infuriate her. So he said: "Damn Angie, your glasses are so thick that I bet when you look at a road map, you can see the people driving in their cars and waving back at out you and shit!"

And that was just enough for her to hear to do what she did next. Even Earlene couldn't believe what this soft-spoken, highly patient little girl did, but it happened. Angie turned into a fireball. She exploded across that table like she had been shot out of a cannon and knocked A.J. out of his chair.

Then she grabbed him by his head and banged it on the floor. The surprise from the attack had him in shock, and after a good seven or eight good raps on the floor with his head, they pulled her off him.

Well, Mrs. Walker heard all the banging on the floor from the basement. So, she ran up the steps and opened the door to see everybody standing around in a circle looking down at the floor. A.J. was lying on the floor on his back with his eyes rolled back in his head. Mrs. Walker looked at him and looked up and around at all the innocent faces and said: "Um Hum, who kicked his ass this time?"

CHAPTER NINE

THE HOG CALLING

Over the next few days, they got a good taste of Aunt Ella's disposition and her relentless attempt to discipline them. And as such, she put together a cleaning crew and assigned them specific work duties. That meant washing the walls, mopping the floor, washing the dishes, and cleaning the oatmeal off the furniture.

She had a profound way of getting her irreversible point across to them, and in a few words, it boiled down to letting them know that "They Couldn't Shit the Shitter." And, on top of that, she held them responsible for respecting each other, and her house, (or you'll answer to me if any of this dumb shit continues to go on!)

On a different note, Samantha was a long way from being happy. She was getting home sick. She was waiting for her Grandma to call like she had promised, but she hadn't heard anything from her yet. Especially when the (super players) Ernie and Monty kept hogging the phone. They had it tied up most of the time and her grandma may have called and not have been able to get through she thought. But she always kept an open ear to hear the phone ring just in case.

Other than that, while everyone else ran around the house like chickens in a barnyard, she made Rah-Mel her new friend. Every morning after breakfast she took her left over table scraps out back and fed them to him. And as unbelievable as it seemed, sometimes she'd sit down next to his cage and read to him out of her story book. Nobody had ever saw anyone calm Rah-Mel down the way she did. It was highly unusual; however, the two of them could communicate like bosom buddies.

Furthermore, Uncle Riley had gotten to a point where he had developed a rapport with Samantha. There was no doubt about it being because of the affect she had on Rah-Mel. It tickled him to pieces to see the way they got along. Therefore, he let her get away with just about anything.

The other knuckleheads in the house were a different story. To him, they were a bunch of contemptible assholes. He found that out after he almost broke his leg slipping on a pile of oatmeal that had oozed up from the kitchen floor. Those little wiseasses just applauded like he was James Brown on stage doing the splits. But he never lost his cool, and he rarely, if ever got upset, yelled, or shouted at any of them.

Anyway, it had been two full weeks since the kids had been there, and Uncle Riley rarely notice them, because most of the time he was up early in the morning underneath the hood of a car. And this was the particular day that his hard work paid off. It was the weekend before the 4th of July holiday, and he needed a good car up and running. It wasn't bran new, neither was it an ugly piece of junk, but it was a rarely used station wagon with good tires and it would do the job.

Uncle Riley had an Army buddy living in the country that raised hogs on his farm. Every year at this time he'd ride out to have him slaughter and dress a couple for him and fixing up that big blue station wagon gave him plenty of room to bring home his haul in one trip.

Anyway, it rained all night long and well into the afternoon that day. Uncle Riley and Alvin were up at 6:00 that morning and were ready to go at 7:00. Furthermore, some of the kids were up as well and they wanted to go with them. So, they all piled in the station wagon, not knowing the extent of the drive, yet relieved to get out the house for a while.

A road filled with fog was in front of them and there was a dark cloudy sky above.

The Johnson farm was in the next county on the outskirts of the city of Hamilton. It was an hour drive through the winding country roads along the Great Miami River, and they were packed in the back seat like sardines; A.J., D.A., Chunk, Popsicle, and Leon. They had no idea that it would take as long as it took to get where they were going. Samantha was in the car too. She was the only girl, but she was wide awake, and proved that she was as sharp as a tack, by using her wily wit to talk Uncle Riley out of the window seat. He had to ride shotgun while Alvin did the driving.

Aunt Ella was up too, but not ready to go just yet. She was going to have her brother, Joel drive the church bus and bring the rest of the gang out later that morning. She had been invited to pick fresh vegetables from the farmer's garden.

The rain drizzled from beneath the dark clouds during their drive up until the time they arrived at the farmer's house. When they arrived, Alvin and Uncle Riley got out the car and carefully made their way around the puddles of water in the dirt rode and up the muddy driveway to the farmer's door.

By the time they reached the door, old man Johnson was right there to open it. He came out and spoke to them loud boisterous: "Hey Riley, How Y'all Doing? Y'all Ready To Kill These Hogs"? Uncle Riley looked up at the six foot four inch farmer and said: "Hell yeah, Johnson." "Well, he said, come on, follow me."

When A.J. saw his dad and Grandfather walking toward the rear of the house, he and the others got out the car and followed them. They followed them around back and down a grassy slope to a large pig pen. Inside it were two humongous hogs. Their names were Daisy and Lucifer; they stood in the middle of the pen oblivious to what was about to happen to them.

There was no way to prepare these kids for what was going to happen next—especially Samantha. And as such, the farmer wasted no time at all. As soon as they reached the pen he opened the gate and hollered Suey! ... Suey! ... Suey! ..., and the hogs came running toward him. Daisy, the smaller hog got there first, and no sooner than he threw a handful of grain on the ground in front her, she buried her shout in it and greedily devoured it from the mud.

In the following seconds, the farmer aimed his rifle at the top of that hog's head and shot it. The hog fell over dead. It was a gruesome sight to see, and it was a particularly troublesome sight for an eight-year-old girl to see. When Samantha heard the gunfire, she cringed and watched the hog drop to the ground. Then she grabbed a hold of Uncle Riley and buried her face in his jacket.

The rest of the boys were awe struck. The sight of the blood, and the hole in that hog's head was mind boggling to them. Some of them couldn't stomach the sight and threw up right there on the spot. Nevertheless, they hadn't seen anything yet– the count was one down and one to go.

The farmer's two sons were standing nearby, and they tied a rope to Daisy's feet and drug her up the slope to the barn. By this time, Lucifer had retreated to the far side of the pen—snorting and shaking his head back and forth like a rebellious bull. If you could have read his mind you would have thought he was saying, (You're Not going to Get Me That Easy). He was every bit of 100 pounds heavier than Daisy and meaner than Black Rhino.

However, the timing of Lucifer's fate was extraordinary. Luckily for him, but unfortunate for them; the farmer had used his last shell when he shot Daisy. The farmer nor his sons could make the drive right then, and it was an hour drive to the closest ammo store in town, so, it turned out that the farmer's wife was the only one capable of making the drive at that time.

Meanwhile, back at the barn, the farmer's teenage sons, Jake and Jerome, went through the process of tying the hog to a meat hook and raising it on a pulley hanging on a rafter in the barn's ceiling. Off to the side, a fifty-gallon barrel of scalding hot water was being heated by a blazing hot fire underneath it.

So, once again, everyone gathered around to see the next gruesome sight. Samantha and her fearless five cousins where about to see something that would make a lasting memory in their minds. They had never seen anything like this before, but it was too late to back down now.

Anyway, it was just like watching a scene from a horror movie. The farmer walked up to the hog with his hunting knife in his hand and raised it high in front of the hog's belly and cut that hog wide open. Next, they witnessed the sight of blood, guts, and gore falling out of it and piling up on the ground right in front of them. Samantha gasped and covered her face with her hands. The reaction to the sight overwhelmed her to the point of tears and she ran to the car, locked the doors and refused to talk to anyone for the rest of the day.

On the flip side, the five amigos hollered when the saw the disgusting sight and tried to refrain from throwing up what little they had left in their stomachs. But they still had to run out of the barn to get away from the sight of it. And as such, the farmer's boys get a big kick out of their reaction, they laughed and laughed, and laughed at them. Nevertheless, they lowered the hog into the barrel of scalding hot water to remove the hair from its hide, and after that, they skinned it and to cut it into different parts.

Soon afterwards, Aunt Ella and the rest of the girls showed up; with the exception of Ernie, Monty, Big Lee and Leroy, who were nowhere to be found when they were leaving, everyone else was there.

Joel went out of his way to make this hour long drive for them, and the only thing he got out of it was a reminder about the harsh reality of living in the country.

Anyway, with all of that over and done, Uncle Riley was getting restless. He wanted that other hog, and he wanted it now. The farmer's wife hadn't returned yet with the shells and he was ready do just about anything to kill that hog. So, as the minutes passed by, one of the farmer's sons mentioned using a sledgehammer to knock the hog unconscious and then cutting its throat so it would bleed to death. Well, it didn't take long for Uncle Riley to go along with that idea. And sure enough, with the farmer's approval, that's exactly what they set out to do.

Well, it stopped raining, the sun was high in the sky and it was hot and humid. Aunt Ella and the girls were there right on time to pick whatever, and as much she wanted from the farmer's garden. However, as soon as they stepped off the bus, the smell coming from the barn was awful. It was too much for them to handle. Therefore. a permanent frown was etched on their faces because of the disgusting smell. Nevertheless, the smell got a little better as soon as they started picking vegetables from the garden. And as such, they all did their part in the garden. However, the real excitement was just beginning down at the pig pen.

So, with no more thought about the matter, the mission began. The lineup went as such. Uncle Riley was first on deck to wield that 20-pound sledgehammer. However, he didn't know about, Lucifer. He wasn't the typical type of hog. He was more of a wild boar with a heightened sense for survival, and he wasn't about to go down without a fight, and that's a fact they all soon came to realize.

Anyway, Uncle Riley picked up that 20-pound sledgehammer and went head hunting, and in his eagerness to kill that hog, get it dressed and back home he made a foolish mistake before anybody could stop him. He stood on the top rail of that fence directly behind that hog and took a wild swing at the back of his head. Well, if he were on an Olympic swim team, he would've scored all tens. Because when he swung at Lucifer's head he missed; he flipped and did a head over heels summersault and landed face first in a pile of hog shit.

Everybody thought that hog had eyes in the back of his head. Lucifer scampered away just as Uncle Riley was about to hit him. The only logical reason they could figure was because of the sun casting a shadow when he stood on that fence directly behind him.

Anyway, it was a Kodak camera moment made everybody laugh. And from that moment on, Uncle Riley had to learn how to live with the new the farmer gave him, "Old Shit Face."

The next slugger on deck was Alvin. He helped his daddy up; got him out of the mud, and out of the pig pen, and then he got in the pen and squared off with Lucifer. The other boys were spread out all around the outside of the pen. A.J. and Chunk were at one end; Popsicle, D.A., and Leon were at the other end, and the farmer's sons, Jake and Jerome were on opposite sides of the pen.

Then they all started shouting and banging on the rails to distract the hog and get its attention so Alvin could get a chance to surprised attack it. That's when Lucifer began squealing, and snorting, and shaking his head back and forth. And as they got louder– the madder that hog got. But Lucifer never took his eyes off Alvin—he stood there in the middle of that muddy pen staring him down.

Well, all of a sudden Lucifer took off running. He headed toward Alvin like he was a practice dummy on a football field, but Alvin didn't back down. He stood his ground like a brave fearless hero.

So, when the hog got close enough, he took a superhero swing at him, and he missed. Likewise, the weight of that sledgehammer and the force behind his swing spent him around so fast and so far, that it was impossible for him to stop. He wound up with his back to the hog, and before he knew it, Lucifer's nose was halfway up Alvin's ass. It had him pent against the fence hollering: "Somebody Get This Motherfucker Off Of Me!"

After that, and to everyone's surprise, A.J. jumped in the pen to help his dad. Alvin was still at the other end of the pen trying to get Lucifer from ramming him in his ass, and A.J. was running to his rescue. But suddenly, Lucifer backed up off Alvin, and turned around and spotted A.J. running toward him.

Well, it was right at that moment when A. J's bravery fell short. He saw Lucifer back up off his dad and tried his best to stop and change directions, but the manure laden mud didn't make it easy. And he slipped, slid, and holler like a bitch when he saw Lucifer coming towards him.

In a matter of seconds Lucifer had his snout buried between A.J.'s hind legs, and he picked him up and tossed him in the air like a rag doll. By the time A.J. fell back down to earth, Little Walter and Popsicle were inside the pen dragging his muddy, mangled body toward the fence before Lucifer could do any more damage to him.

This incredible hog was a monster. It was just like the farmer said—He's a mean sum-bitch. That hog fought them like a warrior. Walter was on one side of A.J. swinging a tree branch at the hog every time it came near, and Popsicle was on his other side with his switchblade opened and swinging it at him like he was in a gang fight.

While all of this was going on, that ganja smoking, Leon was behind the fence putting his supervisory skills to work. He and D.A. were shouting out instructions to the both of them–while at the same time, sucking and puffin on a joint. D.A. said: "That's right, pull him over here, I got him. Hurry up! Ut Oh! Here he comes again. Hit him in the head, Walter—show that big ole rascal how Y'all do it in the ATL. Leon. said: Popsicle, watch out—you better cut him next time. Here he comes again, Pop. Cut him, quick now, Popsicle. Awe, shit, you missed again. Ehee, heeheeheehee Ehee, heeheeheeheeheehe … That's all right. Try it again!"

Then Leon took a toke from the joint and nonchalantly said: "Y'all gonna feel a lot better after y'all smoke some of this 'Scrilla': Ehee, heeheeheeheeheeheehee …"

Interestingly enough, Uncle Joel wasn't far off. He was observing the (Massacre at The Comedy Corral) from the barn. But he eventually walked down to the pen to see what all the drama was about. And, Uncle Joel being Uncle Joel; he wound up smoking that bomb ass scrilla they were hitting. And as such, he wound up giving his expert supervisory advice.

Well, soon enough, Walter and Popsicle had pulled A.J. to safety, and A.J. was on the other side of the pen—fussing, cussing, and selling wolf-tickets to the hog. Well, at that time, the farmer's wife finally showed up. They heard her yelling down to the farmer that she had made it back with the rifle shells.

And as soon as he got them, he got Jake and Jerome to stop laughing, and told them to get the ropes, and they went to work doing their job the way they were taught.

They looked like two rodeo cowboys. They both threw a lasso around Lucifer's head from opposite sides of the pen and tied the end of their ropes to the side of the pen so he couldn't move one way or the other. Then, old man Johnson opened the gate, walked up to that hog, took aim and shot him in the head two times. But, Uncle Riley was still furious about what that hog did to him. So, after that, he snatched the rifle out of Johnson's hands; he took aim at that hog's head and shot him four more times. Then he looked down at dead hog and spit on him and said: "You Rotten Motherfucker!"

After that, and surprised at what had just happened, Jake, Jerome and the farmer stared at Riley for a long time with a look that was said: (That Nigga's Crazy).

CHAPTER TEN

THE COWMAN COM-ETH

It was half-past noon, and the sun radiated beams of heat that not only dried the ground it also dried the mud mixed manure on A.J.'s clothes. So, Leon let him know, flat out that: "You Smell Like Shit, A.J."

A.J. could have gone without hearing that remark for the rest of the day because it pissed him off, and it started an extended argument that ended with the apparent fact that a hog had just assaulted him. Nevertheless, it still didn't change the fact that he still "smelled like shit," and he needed to put some water on that shit.

Anyway, after A.J. calmed down, he saw his dad and Grandfather on the side of the farmer's house using the water hose to wash up. But, instead of waiting for them to finish, he saw Jake and Jerome coming from the barn and asked them if there another place where we can wash up. Well, Jake and his brother stopped what they were doing and looked at each other with a conniving grin on their faces. Then, Jake turned and said: "Yeah, there's a creek down that hill over there where you can wash up, but you better watch out for the cowman." And a split-second later, Jerome said: "Yeah, you can wash off down there, but if the cowman catches you, He'll Fuck You Dry!" Then they started laughing like a couple of criminally insane psychopaths.

Well, they heard what Jake and Jerome said, but, in a way, they didn't hear them, and with A.J. being the type of know-it-all leader he was, he said: "Man, Forget those Fools. Those Hillbillies are just trying to scare us." So, they reluctantly played follow the leader and found a way down that hill.

They came to a cliff where there was a fifty-foot drop-off. There was a stream of water at the bottom that ran into a larger body of water. But it was nothing like the boys thought it would be. It was a really large body of water— from one end to as far as they could see.

Anyway, they stopped for a minute and searched for a way to get to the bottom, and sure enough, about twenty feet to the left of them, they saw an entrance to a trail that would lead them down the hill. So, they followed the path down to the bottom to the front of a small body of water, and there were trees and wildlife all around them.

So, funkier than fearful of the wildlife, A.J., Chunk, and Popsicle waded in a shallow section of the water and rinsed their clothes and bodies off.

While they were doing that, D.A and Leon had a rock skipping contest. And as such, D.A. boasted that he was the best with nine consecutive skips. But, right after their shit-tism in the water, A.J, Chunk, and Popsicle got in on a piece of the action to see if they could beat his record. And, of course, the contest resulted in all of them arguing and claiming to be the winner.

After that, Chunk was the first one to notice a tire-swing hanging from some ropes in the trees. And no sooner than he saw it; he was the first one to test the water. Furthermore, fifty or so yards away from them, there was a boardwalk. It was barely noticeable, but it was sticking out from the bank. And to make things complete, there was a homemade raft with three tire-inner-tubes sitting on top of it.

Well, Chunk didn't waste any time at all. He ran up the hill and slid into one of those tire-swings, and belted out a loud Mississippi River-rat yell while he was swinging out over the middle of that water. Then he slipped out of the tire and plunged into that lake like a Navy rescue diver.

This act of reckless fun appealed to D.A. so much that he grabbed the tire-Swing next and took it out for a ride in the water. And, by sheer accident, his big, size fifteen foot made contact with the side of A.J.'s shoulder when he was swinging past him. It knocked him off balance just enough to push him into Popsicle. But, it didn't stop there; it created a domino effect that resulted in Popsicle losing his balance and bumping into Leon, and all three of them wound up in the water.

Well, Leon was so high and paranoid when he fell in the water that he started hollering like a schoolgirl. He immediately started splashing around and shouting: "Help! I can't swim, I can't swim. Awe. ... shit, I'm gonna drown, I'm gonna drown!"

But, Popsicle and A.J. were in the water right next to him when he fell in, and when they felt their feet touch the bottom of the lake, they stood up and told him to: "Stand up Fool. It's just in four feet of water."

Anyway, after the cool water neutralized their hot bodies, they started having fun. Chunk and D.A were up for the downstroke. They had all their clothes off except their draws, and they swam down to the raft tied to the boardwalk, and before long, they were standing on top of the log-tied vessel navigating it back toward the other boys. When they reached them, they tossed them a tire inner-tube, and the next thing you know, they ventured further down that long, winding stream on an expedition into the abyss.

So, foot pedaling on inner-tubes and pole-pushing a homemade raft, they were suddenly a good quarter-mile downstream, with no end in sight. They traveled through a narrow corridor with towering mud and clay banked cliffs on one side; on the other side was a largely populated brush-filled body of land and trees. Everything seemed to be so serene, undisturbed, and mysterious.

But, as they traveled a little further downstream, they saw a lot of dead fish floating in the water, and the further downstream they went, the more dead fish they saw—laying on the bank rotting with the middle halfway eaten out of them.

After traveling a few yards further, they noticed strange-looking footprints in the mud on the bank, and all of a sudden, Chunk saw something moving in the brush along the shore. He couldn't make out what it was, but he noticed that it was moving in their direction. He told D.A., and he told the rest of the guys, but they didn't see anything.

Right after that, things got spooky. The water started flowing faster, and they kept moving downstream faster and faster. It felt like they were headed for a waterfall up ahead. That's when they immediately decided to head back.

However, following that decision, a tremendous cloud burst, and the rain poured down on them. The sky turned black; Marble size raindrops pounded the water. Then a strong, violent wind appeared to impede their effort to get back to where they started. Naturally, they panicked, which led to them pedaling those inner-tubes and pushing that raft harder and faster.

Eventually, they started moving again at a robust and steady pace, but then they heard the loud sound of leaves rustling and tree branches cracking in the brush. D.A. and Chunk kept looking back to see what was following them, but it was hard to see anything through the drenching rain and the heavily populated brush on the shore.

Then they saw a frightening sight. D.A. and Chunk saw a hairy, nasty looking man-like creature standing on the shore, and their first thought was that it was a Big Foot. Its body was half-hidden in the brush as it stood there on the bank, glaring at them with blood-red eyes—growling and grumbling like some crazed beast.

Then, all of a sudden, they yelled: "Bigfoot! It's a Bigfoot following us Y'all! Y'all its a Bigfoot following us!" Right afterward, they heard thunder rumbling, and immediately following that, they heard a sound that they had never heard before. It sounded like a sick cow mooing in pain, but it was a hundred times louder than a normal cow's mooing, and it went on and on and on.

But, when the frightening sound finally stopped, they all saw it. It looked like a creature from hell– unbelievably grotesque.

However, this time it rose up on two hind legs and bolstered out another loud, painful sounding cry that made their assholes pucker and piss run down their leg.

And during that brief time, A.J. made an acute observation. He said: "Hey Chunk., how many legs does a Bigfoot have"? Chunk said two. Then A.J. took another long hard look at it and said: "That Mutha-fucka got Four Legs! That ain't no Goddamn Bigfoot!" "Lets Get The Fuck Out Of Here"!

The first thought that crossed their minds was that (now I know what those two country sons-of-a- bitches were laughing about).

D.A. And Chunk immediately jumped off the raft into the water, and all of their narrow asses took off swimming like a swarm of dolphins at sea. But, when they took off, so did that cowman—in a gallop along the shore—keeping up with their every stroke.

Then it let out yet another long, horrendous, painful sounding cry that was so loud it vibrated the walls in that canyon– mud and clay started falling off in huge chunks– so large they rippled the water onto the bank. However, they eventually made it back to where they started from. And as quick as they got there, they were even quicker about grabbing their clothes and running up that hill– slipping and sliding their way to the top.

The terror-stricken look on their faces said it all. They had all saw what they saw, but somehow none of them could find the right words to describe what they saw. And with dilated eyes and jaw-dropping mouths, that same look of shock stayed on their faces the rest of the way home.

But the final straw was seeing those two crazy-ass farm boys before they pulled off. Jake and Jerome showed up just in time to say good-bye. And when they heard their voices from the back seat, they turned around and saw them waving and grinning like the two Goonies from a Funny-Farm that they were.

CHAPTER ELEVEN

FUNK HITS THE FAN/SEXUAL HEALING

They got home right as the bright orange sun was sinking to the horizon; everyone was tired from the drive and glad to be home. They got off the bus and out of the car and immediately began taking their fruits of labor in the house. But, instead of helping unload the packages of meat from the station wagon and taking them to the basement door with the other boys, A.J. went straight to his Grandma to help her off the bus.

A.J. walked her to the back door and helped carry a bag of collard greens and potatoes. He set the bags on the kitchen table and turned on the kitchen light. But, when he turned around to head back out the door, he heard strange noises coming from the front room. Through the sound of silence, he listened to the distinctive sound of moans and groans and smelt a smell all too familiar to him.

As he stopped to listen more intently, he suddenly remembered that the rest of the boys were still at home. Mrs. Walker had stopped what she was doing and froze like a statue in the middle of the kitchen floor—she was listening to the same sounds, and she had her nose in the air like a radar detector. She, too, was trying to figure out where she had smelt that funky smell before; and, her senses quickly concluded that something devilish was going on in her house.

However, before she could set out to get to the bottom of it, A.J. had already busted a move to the front room to deliver a message to the horny lovers. He knew that the moaning and groaning sounds he heard weren't coming from the television, and he definitely knew what pussy smelled like. So, when he got to the front room, he looked inside and saw just what he expected to see. Ernie and Monty were getting it on with two super-freaks. They were all half-naked—Knocking Boots. Kissing, humping and grinding; moaning and groaning.

There were empty wine cooler bottles and beer cans everywhere; on the table and floor; half-smoked blunts were in the ashtray; a deck of cards lay open and half scattered all over the table, and pretzels and potato chips were on the floor.

Anyway, he whispered to them, "Hey, you damn fools, Grandma is in the other room. You better get them the Hell out of here!" But, by the time A J had finished warning them, he looked up and saw his Grandma standing in front of him. She gave him a scornful glare after he tried to block her from going into the living room and told him to "Move out the way!"

When she looked inside, and she could hardly believe what she saw. Visions of Sodom and Gomorrah immediately flashed through her mind, and she went into a conniption–she screamed and shouted: "Oh lord help me Jesus! Help me Jesus! Oh God just take me, take me, God! Right Now! Right Now, take me lord! take me now …!"

All of a sudden, she got so light-headed that she fainted, and all three-hundred pounds of her robust body fell towards A.J. He was so shocked when she fell that he screamed for help at the top of his lungs. He desperately tried to hold her up the best he could, but she was too much woman for his weak little arms to handle, and it seemed like hours to him, but luckily, some of the girls came running to his rescue and helped him set her down in a chair.

Ernie and Monty jumped up and were rushing to put their draws back on. And before she regained consciousness. Then they rushed to clean up the living room. They tried as fast as they could to remove all the trash and debris around them before she woke up and before the funk hit the fan.

Well, by the time the two girls had gotten dressed, in their hast to get out the front door, Kim recognized one of the girls. "Peaches, she said, is that you?" Peaches turned away with a sheepish look on her face and didn't answer, but Kim walked up to her to get a closer look and said: "Yeah, that is you!" When Earlene saw her, she wasn't surprised at all. She knew that Ernie had the hots for her ever since church last Sunday. And as such, her history of knowing Peaches and seeing her now spoke volumes. "Yeah, that's that two-dollar ho." And Angie said: "Yeah. That's the girl from church who's always trying to act all sanctified.

Peaches was highly offended by their snide comments, so she blasted back, saying, "I ain't no Ho, Bitch!" But before Angie and Earlene could tune her ass up, Ernie jumped in to defend her:

"Leave her alone, Y'all always trying to start some trouble." But it didn't end there.

"I know you didn't call me a Bitch—Bitch! You're out here running around with this Slut, Yolanda. The whole world knows she's a community property whore. And you ain't nothing but a goodie-two-shoe acting ho." Then Earlene looked at Kim and Angie and said, "Let's kick their Asses Y'all!

Fortunately, and just in time, Grandma regained consciousness and was tuned into the last statement Earlene made. She quickly came to her senses. She slowly pushed her 6- foot frame out of the chair and got to her feet. She said: "If anybody's going to do any Ass Kicking around here it's going to be Me!"

That's when everybody in the room tried to leave—they all headed for the door. But, Mrs. Walker caught them off guard. She blew out a loud, crisp command whistle to stop. She said: "Everybody Freeze! Freeze! get back in here! I ain't through with y'all yet." So, when she got them back in the house, she cross-examined them like a prosecuting attorney.

She turned to Ernie and said: "What's going on here?" Ernie started babbling, "Ain't nothing going on, Grandma. We was just having some fun playing cards, that's all." She said, "Is that why I saw beer cans and wine bottles all over my living room? Boy, do you think I'm a fool? And you been smoking reefer in my house too!"

She paused in silence for a moment, and then she asked him: "Boy, don't you have one a baby already? And, I heard you got another girl pregnant!" "Naw, Grandma, that baby ain't mine." "Boy, shut up. Its the same old story on a different day with you.

You kids are just babies—Babies making Babies—that's all you are—Babies making Babies. You're too young to be fornicating, especially in my house!"

"You're fifteen years old, boy, and you're gonna have two babies to take care of before you're eighteen. You don't have a job, a pot to piss in, or a window to throw it out of. Boy, it's time to get something on your mind—and the same goes for you Monty."

Ernie was speechless, but he did manage to tell his Grandma that he was sorry, and there was no doubt that he was embarrassed. He just took what his Grandmother had to say and held his head down like he was ashamed.

Next, standing in front of her with scraggly hair and wrinkled blouses, were the two girls. She looked them over and said: "Yolanda, what in the Hell are you two doing in my house. You're from the West End—down on 14th street. Don't think I don't know who you are—I know your mama, (but only the lord knows who your daddy is, she mumbled) And you! Ain't you Reverend Kimble's daughter?"

Peaches held her head up and spoke softly, "Yes Mam." Mrs. Walker shook her head and mumbled to herself, "well -- lord have mercy, ain't this a blip. I know your mama would whoop your ass if she knew you were over here."

Then she laid down the law. "Now, here this," she said, "These boys are here to learn how to live a Christian life and learn lessons from the Bible—not the kind of lessons you want to teach them. They're going to know who they are and where they come from when they leave this house. "Now, if I catch nan one of you in my house again without my permission, you're gonna be sucking your supper through a plastic straw for the rest of your natural life. Got it! Now go on, get out of here!"

Well, not long after the girls made their way out the front door, Lee and Leroy came stumbling through. They had been gone all day scouting the neighborhood, meeting new people, and getting their swerve on. Fortunately, Aunt Ella wasn't around to smell their distilled alcoholic breath. And boy, did they have some stories to tell.

However, it was getting late, and all of them were hungry. So, after they ate their bologna and government cheese sandwich and washed it down with a big glass of Kool-Aid, they all had a chance to talk about their adventuresome day.

They matched stories about their encounter with the half-man/half-cow; Ernie and Monty boasted about the Freaky Deaky time they had with Peaches and Yolanda, and Lee and Leroy talked about the people they met, including their should-haves, would-haves, could-haves, and what they actually did.

But, to put a cap on the night, A.J told them a joke about a quadriplegic girl in a wheelchair. He said: "There was this quadriplegic girl (she didn't have any legs or arms), and she was sitting in a wheelchair next to a swimming pool. A friend of hers heard her crying one day and walked up to her and asked her why she was crying. The girl told him, "because don't nobody love me," and the friend told her that he loved her, and she smiled and cheered up. And the next day, the friend saw her sitting by the pool crying again. So, he asked her what she was crying about now. And the girl said, "because don't nobody ever kiss me." So, the friend kisses her, and she smiles and cheers up. So, the day after that, the friend sees her sitting by the pool crying again. So, he asked her, "what are you crying about today." And the girl says, "because don't nobody ever fuck me." So, the friend grabs hold of the girl's wheelchair and rolls her over to the deep end of the pool and pushes her ass in the water, and he says: "You're Fucked Now!"

CHAPTER TWELVE

THE STAR-SPANGLED EXPLOSION

After a long, restful night of sleep, the next morning, the sound of gunfire riddled through the neighborhood streets. Today was the 4th of July, and either that sudden burst of gunfire was an indication of the country's celebration of independence or a drive-by shooting. Either way, it served as an alarm clock to get started with a day of festivities.

The first one up—other than Aunt Ella and Uncle Riley was Samantha, as usual. She had gotten in the habit of getting up early to eat breakfast and to feed her leftover scraps to Rah-Mel, but today her duty included helping in the kitchen.

Today was a big day for the entire family, and everyone in the house was needed to help get things ready for the backyard cookout. Mrs. Walker had put several-frozen slabs of ribs and whole chickens in the kitchen sink last night, and Uncle Riley and Alvin were in the backyard filling up a fifty-gallon barrel grill with wood and charcoal.

Decisions had to be made as to who would be helping her

prepare the food and clean the house—both inside and outside. In addition to those duties, there were still a dozen or more things to do.

So, to get this party started right, Alvin popped opened the trunk of his car and pumped up the volume on his CD player; he played his "James Brown" to get in the groove. However, the Super Soul groove that James Brown put him in was eventually overturned by a vote to change to a Hip-Hop groove. Thus, Tu Pac, Biggie, and Snoop-Dog were the preferred artist of choice. And likewise, the good spirits that the music put them in made it easier for them to clean, cook, sing, and dance through the whole shebang. There was no doubt that the music brought them closer together, and in a way that they all bonded as families should. And naturally, seeing that sight made Mrs. Walker very happy.

The Drama Begins

It took a couple of hours before most of the hard work was done. Tables were set up with plastic table clothes on them and folding chairs underneath them. Japanese lanterns were strung up across the yard from one end to the other. Food was cooking in the oven and on top of the stove, and Uncle Riley and Alvin were taking turns cooking on the grill while quenching their thirst with a 12-pack of ice-cold beer.

As soon as the girls had all the work was done inside, they went outside to chill with the boys, and for the first time, they were all getting along and having fun together. But, as they all gathered around the picnic table waiting on a cool breeze to come their way—there was none, and they were getting hot, sweaty, and thirsty. So, after sitting in the same spot for several minutes, with the breeze refusing to come, they moved the table under a tree for shade. However, their final idea to cool off was to get ice-balls from the deep freezer in the basement.

Well, that worked for a minute, but it wasn't enough to completely cool off their hot body temperatures. And as such, another option popped into the minds of two frivolous scamps. A.J. and Chunk suddenly disappeared from the group but were later spotted peeping out the third-floor window. A without a doubt, a minute or two later, those two scoundrels "set it off."

The first throw was a direct hit. A.J. busted his dad in the back of his head with a water balloon. Then Chunk raised up and threw the next one. It was a direct hit, too—right in his Grandpa Riley's chest. After they hit them, they laid back down on the floor to get out of sight and laughed their devilish little asses off. The other kids were stunned when they saw what happened, but, at the same time, they were amused to the point of laughter.

Although, not so amused, was Alvin and Uncle Riley. Alvin was pissed, and so was his dad. Alvin grabbed the back of his head and shouted, "Son-of-a-bitch!" his first thought was that he had got shot, but he soon realized that it was water on his head— not blood. And, Uncle Riley thought it was all over for his ass too, but he saw the busted balloon laying on the ground in front of him and realized that someone was up to some shit.

But it didn't stop there. It seems that those two little shits had been planning this all night long. They had a washtub filled with water balloons set aside for this moment. So, with all fun intended, they continued their disruptive distribution process by bombing whoever they could from the third-floor window.

Those two water-balloon assassins worked from that third-floor window with the skill, precision, and tenacity of two professional snipers. They would pop-up, throw their balloon, hit their target, and get back down and out of sight so that no-one could identify which one of them hit them.

Earlene was next to feel the sting of a balloon bursting on her back. She cringed from the cold water running down her back and shouted: "Oh, Hell No!" Then Kim took two hits to the back of her head that knocked her into a state of double-vision. It had her staggering back and forth so much that she fell on Angie.

Right after that, they heard Leon laughing like a hyena— but not for long. The aerial precision displayed next compelled D.A. and Popsicle to laugh at Leon. Because just then, he was double-attacked. Chunk threw a balloon that screw-balled Leon right between his teeth, and A.J backed him up with a balloon that busted right upside his head.

Thus, as the terrorist balloon threats continued, the civilian population below scattered and scrambled around in a frenzy. They were helplessly at the mercy of the attackers and forced to use garbage-can tops to ward off the incoming barrage of balloons.

However, just like two commanders of a task force, Uncle Riley and Alvin came up with a plan to fight back. Alvin ran to his car and pulled out their secret weapon. Inside the large paper bag that he brought back with him were all kinds of fireworks—firecrackers, cherry-bombs, roman-candles, sparklers, and M-80's—the closest explosive to dynamite that can be legally sold as a commercial commodity.

Well, with no time wasted, and like two foot-soldiers on a combat mission, they quickly attacked the third-floor window. The first assault came from a round of firecrackers. Uncle Riley manned the fire from his lighter while Alvin lit a stringer of 50 of the volatile projectiles and skillfully tossed them through the third-floor window.

Immediately after landing on the floor between the two insurgents, the sound from that room resonated like machine-gun fire. Scared shit-less, A.J. and Chunk hit the floor and stayed there until it was over. Even Rah-Mel went berserk. He was climbing the walls of his cage when he heard the firecrackers exploding in rapid succession.

But that assault alone didn't get those two courageous soldiers to deviate from their established course of action one iota; it only intensified their savage instinct to vilify their subjects even more. So, with wild abandon, they pummeled one water-bomb after another directly beneath the window in a ceaseless effort to force the two hostiles (Uncle Riley and Alvin) into a new position.

Their counter-assault was devastating. It was a gloriously magnificent defeat that could have been recorded in the logbook of water-balloon history. There are no words that can describe the assault, other than to say that no self-respecting duck would have been caught in a situation of this magnitude. Alvin and his dad were soaked from head to toe.

The others witnessed this brutal assault go on right in front of them, and from then on, a sense of retaliation overwhelmed all of them. Because now, it was an all-out war.

Ernie and Monty hooked up the garden hose lying at the bottom of the basement door and attached a spray nozzle to the other end of it; it was definitely going to be needed if this battle was going to continue on this level. D.A. Leon and Popsicle were grabbing any and everything that they could find on the battlefield ground to throw at them—sticks, bottles, and rocks.

Half of the girls went on a tactical mission up the stairs to the third floor to surprise attack and beat the hell out of them, and the other half stood on the ground selling wolf-tickets trying to draw their fire so Ernie and Monty could blast them with the hose.

Nonetheless, in between and in the meantime, Uncle Riley and Alvin had made it to a safe haven behind the huge Maple tree beside the grill. Mad as hell, sopping wet, and dripping with nullification from the mouth, Uncle Riley opened that bag of fireworks and looked inside for something that would blast their asses to the sky.

He said, "Give me those goddamn m-80's!" Alvin said, damn, daddy! You're going to blow the whole damn house down!" Uncle Riley said, "I don't give a shit. Do you see what those little Mutha-fuckers did to me? I'll blow those little sum-bitches to kingdom come. Tell the Lord to meet em in heaven; cause I'm gonna cover their asses with dirt when I'm through em".

A.J. and Chunk were unaware of their new strategy; nonetheless, Alvin and Uncle Riley moved into a position to perpetuate their new assault. They cautiously approached the third- floor window to a point where they knew the projectiles would enter the window without obstruction and deliver the greatest impact. They made it to the house and positioned themselves; undetected by neither of the balloon-bombing bandits. Seconds later-- 5,4.3,2.1—pssssssst—pssssst--swish ... -ta—dump, ta—dump.

The miniature explosive packs landed in the middle of the floor, hissing like two cobras. A.J. and Chunk saw both of the mini-charged explosives land on the floor, and their eyes bulged with fright. Their first thought was to get the hell out of the room. But, the sound of the banging and hollering on the other side of the door from the girls trying to get in let them know that they were in big trouble.

Besides that, the door was blocked by tables, chairs, a dresser, and an old trunk to keep the enemy out.

Well, this was definitely a good time to panic, because after they looked at the door, they looked at each other; then they looked at the open window. And as such, a split-second later, they busted a move towards it.

Well, it looked like a scene right out of an action Jackson movie after that, those two m-80's went "KA-Boom! KA-Bam" and the momentum they had running toward the window was intensified by the thrust of the explosion. It sent them flying out of the third-floor window, hollering through an unbelievable flight "Awe ... ... Shit ... ...,!" looking like two sky-divers without parachutes. Just the same, they were very lucky to have made it all the way to the maple tree branches in the yard and even more fortunate to have landed on the picnic table that was underneath it.

Anyway, the ground troops were awestruck when they saw A.J.

and Chunk fly through the air and topple down through those tree branches. When they saw the two wounded warrior's lifeless bodies lying there on the table, they thought they were dead. And when Aunt Ella saw the little jackasses laying there in their state of catatonia, she shouted "Oh, Lord Have Mercy! ..." because she thought they were dead too. But her loud shouting must have jolted them back into consciousness because they slowly began moving around.

Well, this was obviously a remarkable feat they just witnessed and one which a few of the Bible-toting cousins thought was a miracle. Therefore, Kim, Angie, and Tamara found it appropriate to praise the Lord and applaud their survival. They were so exuberant and facetiously exalted by their survival that they decided that it was a time to rejoice. So, they all clapped their hands, stomped their feet, and started singing an old Negro Spiritual:

"We gonna jump down, turn around—pick-a-bail of cotton– Jump up jump down—pick-a-bail of hay—Ohh Lordy ... ., Pick-a-bail of cotton—Oh lordy ... ., pick-a-bail of hay ..."

"Me and My Cousins gonna jump down, turn around—pick-a-bail of cotton– Jump up jump down—pick-a-bail of hay—Ohh Lordy ... ., Pick-a-bail of cotton—Ohh lordy ... ., pick-a-bail of hay ..."

Ohh Lordy ... ., Pick-a-bail of cotton—Ohh lordy ... ., pick-a-bail of hay ..."

Ohh Lordy ., Pick-a-bail of cotton—Ohh lordy ... ., pick-a-bail

"We gonna jump down, turn around—pick-a-bail of

cotton– Jump up jump down—pick-a-bail of hay—Oh Lordy ... ., Pick-a-bail of cotton—Oh lordy ... ., pick-a-bail of hay ..."

"Me and My Cousins gonna jump down, turn around—pick-a-bail of cotton– Jump up jump down—pick-a-bail of hay—Oh Lordy ... ., Pick-a-bail of cotton—Oh lordy ... ., pick-a-bail of hay ..."

Oh Lordy ... ., Pick-a-bail of cotton—Oh lordy ... ., pick-a-bail of hay ..."

Oh Lordy ... ., Pick-a-bail of cotton—Oh lordy ... ., pick-a-bail of hay ..."

They sang, clapped their hand, stomped their feet, and strutted around the backyard like they were on an Alabama plantation, right up until the time that Mrs. Walker said, let's eat.

CHAPTER THIRTEEN

THE DRIVE-BY DROP-OFF

Uncle Hump had a raw and sometimes brutal way of speaking his mind. He said what was natural for him to say, and he was shameless after he said what he had to say. But, most of the time, he was a fun-loving, easy-going guy; however, unpredictable.

Well, it completely surprised Mrs. Walker when her "menace-to-society" brother showed up at the cookout. Although this wasn't his intended destination, he wound up there due to a "drive-by-drop off."

He had been a recent passenger in his x-wife's car until he pissed her off. And, things being what they were, while in the vicinity of his sister's house, she barreled down the back alley to where she lived and told him to get the fuck out. After that, she pulled off, kicking back dirt and gravel from beneath her tires, creating a cloud of dust, and at the same time, shouting every obscenity in a Black woman's vocabulary. But as usual, Uncle Hump was cool about it. He just stood there, shrugged his shoulders, and said: "I can't stand your black ass either. You Bitch!"

Folks gave him the nickname 'Hump' because of his reputation for being in brawls in the back-alley's, pool halls, and bars around town. And, more or less, because of the size of the knots on his forehead that wouldn't go away.

Well, soon after his blatant abandonment, he shook the dust from his pant legs, straightened the feather in the brim of his hustler's hat, opened the gate to the backyard, and walked inside, just in time for dinner.

His first stop was at the grill, where he saw a cloud of smoke and Alvin and Uncle Riley burning the last pieces of meat they were cooking. But, before making his entrance, he checked his package with one hand, swung his other arm to the synchronously timed strut that gave him recognition as being a Mack, and went on his way to meet them.

"Hey, what's up, brother-in-law? How you doing, nephew?" "Hey, what's going on Unc, how you been? Uncle Hump said: "nephew: I keep my powder dry, my dick hard, and watch the World Turn' baby; how about you?" Uncle Riley quickly posed the next question: "Nigga, when did they let you out of jail?" Hump said, "Don't you worry about that, nigga, I'm here right now. Signed, sealed, and delivered, Baby! If you 'free your mind, your ass will follow.' That's something that an old country ass nigga like you don't know nothing about." And in the same breath, he held out his hand and said, "let me hold something?" Uncle Riley turned his back on him and said, "Fuck you Nigga!."

All of a sudden, Sparkle jumped on his back and wrapped her arms around his neck. She shouted, "Grandpa". However, Leon wasn't so charmed when he saw his legendary Grandfather. It was an awkward moment for him, and one in which his distinctive laughter wouldn't be heard. From past experiences, he knew that as soon as he showed up, he'd make him another promise, tell another lie, and be gone again. So, he didn't even take the time to be bothered with him.

Aunt Ella was of a similar opinion about her brother. He had been a disappointment in many respects and many times before. She was standing on the porch with an apathetic look on her face when she saw him. When he looked up and saw her sweeping off the porch, he walked over to her and immediately heard the sarcasm in her voice: "Well, well, well, the fugitive has returned." But, being the silky-smooth kind of player he was, he just responded with his special brand of charm. "Now is that any way to talk to your favorite baby brother, Sis? Come on now, wobble your big ass down those steps and show me some love."

Well, as much as she wanted him to feel the disgust she had for him, she made her way down the porch steps and gave him a hug and a kiss. After that, Uncle Hump turned into his fun-loving, playful self and grabbed his great-nieces, one-by-one, and swung them round and round until they couldn't walk straight after he let them go.

He showed his great-nephews his boxing style and sparred with all of them. He playfully threw light punches at them— intentionally landing one or two hard punches now and then to show them that he still had some sting in his punch. But when he landed a stiff blow to Popsicle's chest, Popsicle countered with a hard, right hand to Uncle Hump's jaw and drew blood from the corner of his mouth. And pretending to be upset, Uncle Hump looked at the blood on his hand, stuck his other hand in his back pocket, and playfully said, "Awe Shit! Now I got ta cut ya."

But, quick as a flash, Popsicle flicked open his switchblade, and stood in a ready position, and said, "Bust a move, you old Mutha-Fucka!" But, during that brief moment, Uncle Hump had a flashback; he saw an image of himself standing there doing the exact same thing forty years ago—brave, full of heart, and foolish. So, he laughed and said, "somebody put on some music."

After that, someone put on the music, and the soul-train showdown began. But first, Uncle Hump brought the funk back to town and taught his hip-hop generation of nieces and nephews how to do the bump, the atomic-dog, and the cosmic slop.

Then they started a Soul-Train dance line, and in turn, they showed Uncle Hump how to do their dances. They showed him how to do the wobble, the butterfly, and the cabbage-patch.

Finally, they voted on the 1st, 2nd, and 3rd place winners of the Soul-train line and argued over who did what dance the best. And as such, the fun lasted until sundown, which is when they set off the fireworks.

The Great Escape

As darkness fell, Uncle Riley set off his fireworks, and, all of a sudden, the sound of firecrackers exploding could be heard everywhere. The night sky was illuminated by a colorful rainbow of lights bursting throughout the surrounding neighborhood.

However, barely noticeable, sitting across the ally in a big black Cadillac, were two men with the driver-side window pulled halfway down. As soon as Uncle Hump saw the car sitting there, he ducked down as low as he could get besides the picnic table to get out of sight. And right after the bright sky returned to darkness, he made a B-line for the back door and went inside the house. But, when the night sky was lit up again, the men in the car noticed that Uncle Hump was nowhere in sight.

As it turned out, two men were gangsters from Detroit, and they had been watching the house for some time now. They were after Hump for who knows what reason. Furthermore, immediately following Uncle Hump's sudden disappearance, A.J. was so curious that he followed him to find out what was going on. But, when he got inside the house, Hump suddenly came out of a dark hallway, muffled A. J.'s mouth with his hand and pulled him back into the dark hallway. And in a low, desperate whisper, he asked A.J. if he knew anybody with a car.

Meanwhile, the two men had gotten out of the car and walked up to the backyard fence. They had on black three-piece suits and wore Gangster style fedoras. When they reached the gate, one of the men asked, "Does anybody here know Hump Wilson?" There was a dead silence, and several seconds went by with no answer to his question. So once again, speaking louder, he asked: "Does anybody here know Hump Wilson?" Then Uncle Riley walked toward Rah-Mel's cage in plain view of the men and answered their question with the question: "Who wants to know?"

During that same moment, Alvin took this as a queue to get everybody inside the house. So, he got up and walked toward the house, and at the same time, he told everyone to go inside. And, with little resistance, they felt a stern sense of seriousness in his voice and went inside without questions. So, after everyone was through the door, he walked toward the back of his car, unlocked the trunk, and stood by the side.

Nevertheless, still standing at the fence, the two men were at a loss for words to answer the question Uncle Riley asked them. Therefore, both of them spoke at the same time—each with a different answer, stumbling over the right words to say. And with that being the case, the only reasonable answer they could respond with was that "We're just some old friends of his from out of town, and we wanted to stop by to see how he was doing—that's all."

Well, Uncle Riley and Alvin had already surmised that these two men weren't cops, and they sure as hell weren't his friends. From the way they were dressed, they were either businessmen, or a couple of hit-men after Hump to pay a debt he owed. And for obvious reasons, the latter thought was the correct one.

So, assuming that was the case, Uncle Riley gave them a few profound words of advice. He told them: "Look here, the only thing I'd like to see more than fireworks lighting up in the sky tonight, is the fire I'm gonna light under your asses if you don't get off my Goddamn property, right fucking Now!"

Then he opened the gate to Rah-Mel's cage and shouted the command: "Kill Rah-Mel!" And he took off running towards the fence barking ferociously.

Alvin was leaning against the back end of his car, and as soon as he heard Rah-Mel's barking, he opened the trunk of his car and grabbed his gun, and waited for his daddy to make the next move.

Startled by the sudden surprise, both men reached inside their suit coats and pulled revolvers from their shoulder holsters, and pointed them at Rah-Mel. However, amid this distraction, Uncle Riley had quickly reached inside a compartment on top of Rah-Mel's doghouse and pulled out a 12-gauge shotgun. He had it aimed at the men, and he angrily shouted, "If you shoot my dog, you'll be some dead Mutha-fuckers right where you stand!" Alvin was standing right alongside his daddy with his nine, cocked, loaded, and pointed at both men this time.

Naturally, the gangster's attitudes quickly changed after they saw that the odds were stacked against them, so they nervously muttered, "O k. O k, O k old man—don't shoot—do you hear me, don't shoot, we're leaving– we're leaving right now! Alright!" And it was plain to see that they were as mad as hell from being outmaneuvered, so they hurried back across the alley, got in their car, and drove off.

Anyway, immediately following their hasty departure, A.J was heard coming through the front door. He had taken Uncle Hump out the front door and across the street to a neighbor's house, and accordingly, Uncle Hump promptly finagled him into driving across the river into Kentucky. Anyway, after they witnessed that stressful situation in the backyard, there was a sigh of relief, and a lot of angry words spouted at A.J. when they all realized it was him.

But the worst part of the night was when they saw the long, sad look of disappointment on Sparkle's face, knowing that her Grandfather had left without even saying good-bye. Nevertheless, Leon was used to this sort of thing happening. He knew for sure that his Grandfather was going to be on the run again, and frankly, he didn't give a shit.

CHAPTER FOURTEEN

HOT CONFLICTS

Uncle Hump wasn't seen or heard from for the remainder of the summer. Despite their experience and knowledge of the ordeals and controversy that were a natural part of his life, he was always going to be remembered for bringing them a certain amount of joy at a special time in their lives.

Anyway, as their summertime experience continued, one hot conflict after another continued to occur. Furthermore, the mischief and mayhem pattern that prevailed in this house of reform and Bible education was undoubtedly supplemented by the blazing hot temperature during July; thus, attributing to the extraordinary increase in drama. However, the hot weather cannot diminish the fact that many of these conflicts were a direct result of the vengeful thoughts that a select few family members were harboring against each other.

Aunt Ella wanted these children to be knowledgeable of who their cousins and the immediate family members were. Bringing cousins together for the summer had been done before. It had become a matter of tradition in this family and the process of carrying out a mission to get kids accustomed to going to church.

Therefore, during the next four weeks, these kids attended several churches: a Baptist church, a Methodist church, a Lutheran church, and a Holiness church. Some of them were so tired of going to church that they felt like a group of traveling Jesuits every time they got on that bus.

At times they were bored out of their minds sitting in church all day long. And at times, it seemed like some of the people in the church were giving unbelievable testimonials. Individual members would provide the same testimonial every week about how God intervened in their sons' or daughters' lives and made them miss a plane or a train ride that later crashed with no survivors.

And sometimes the services were so comical that some of the kids couldn't stop laughing. When the preacher used street slang talking to the church's younger members, it had them laughing until tears rolled from their eyes.

Consequently, when it came down to learning lessons in church, the most profound lessons to stick in their minds were that: Methodist preachers were Thunderbird wine drinking alcoholics; Holiness preachers were fried chicken eating, biscuit and gravy sopping gluts; that Baptist preachers were, two-faced, womanizing adulterers, and that the Lutheran church was spooky as hell!

Anyway, when they got back home, it was plain to see that these kids weren't angles. Aunt Ella's big, spacious home had become a place where they could be free and run wild. Thus, their usual mode of behavior resumed its course. Therefore, incidents of mischief and unbelievable pranks were carried on behind Mrs. Walker's back–around the clock.

The first incident to reach 99.9 on the 'mischief meter' occurred on a sweltering, hot afternoon. Popsicle was craving one of those sweet cherry ice-balls in the basement deep-freezer, and as such, he took off on his own, walking through the back hallway toward the basement. Well, his timing couldn't have been better. His archenemy, Kim, the queen of the oatmeal fight, just happened to be in the kitchen–filling up Dixie Cups with Kool-Aid. She placed them on a flat metal pan and was just about ready to take them to the basement.

Well, Popsicle happened to be standing behind the half-opened door watching her through the crack of the door, and naturally, a rotten thought crossed his mind. So, he patiently stood there and watched and waited for her to finish. When she finished, she picked up the pan and slowly walked towards the door without spilling a drop of Kool-Aid: so far, so good. Then, she went through the door and got one foot firmly planted on the first step. But, as soon as she put her other foot on the step, "Wham" Popsicle pushed the door and slammed it against her hefty behind, and it knocked her off balance and sent her tumbling down a flight of twenty steps– screaming at the top of her lungs.

Unfortunately, no-one could hear her screams but Popsicle, and when he did, the rotten creep felt a sense of pleasure and satisfaction. And as far as he was concerned, hearing her yell like that was sweeter than any cherry-ice-ball could have ever been.

The cups of Kool-Aid went flying in the air when she tumbled down that long flight of steps to the cement floor.

The only sounds that could be heard in that basement were the sounds of the wooden steps cracking and her yelling: "Awe ... ... Shit!" Down to the bottom.

Amazingly, the booms and bangs and terror-filled screams didn't escape Samantha's hearing. She was in the backyard with Rah-Mel when she heard the tragic moment transpire. So, she immediately went to the basement window to see what had happened.

She was surprised to see Kim sitting at the bottom step, slumped over in a daze, covered from head to toe with cherry Kool-Aid. But she could tell by her slow movement that she was hurt, and fortunately, she was still alive, so with no-time wasted, she ran to her rescue.

Meanwhile, that black Hearted buzzard inconspicuously fled from the crime scene and ran into D.A. in the next room. He stopped to tell him about his dastardly deed, where they both enjoyed a fiendish laugh about his appalling act of terrorism.

Anyway, Kim and Sam didn't know who was responsible, but they had a strong suspicion, and they knew that it wasn't an accident.

After clearing her head and the crime scene, they brainstormed a plan to determine who was responsible and how to get even.

Meanwhile, the third floor of the house was rocking with the sound of hip-hop music. It was so loud that it blasted through the floor and down the steps where the two co-conspirators were collaborating. When they heard the music, they were ensued by a spirit of exploration, and naturally, feeling emboldened with confidence, they went upstairs to satisfy their curiosity.

When they got there, they walked in to see Danielle and Sparkle smoking Cigarettes and sipping on a pint of Long Island Iced Tea. Deeper still, they were dressed up like "Salt n Pepper" and singing: "What a man, what a man, what a man, what a mighty good man." And from the sound of their slurred singing, you could tell they were drunk. Sparkle was standing in front of a long, stand-up mirror, putting on makeup and jewelry and brushing her hair to match Salt-n-Pepper's style.

But as soon as Danielle saw them, she invited them in. She lounged in a reclining chair with a bottle of iced tea in her hand. Furthermore, she was wearing a short skirt and had one leg cocked up over the chair's arm with her panties showing.

She said, "Hey Popsicle, do you want-a Pop this Thang? I got some chocolate puddin for you, baby. Umm, its and it's sweet too." Then Sparkle started flirting with D.A. She bent over in front of the mirror, wearing tight booty shorts, and began to twerk her behind like it was a bowl of jello. She said: "Hey D.A., do you wanna ride my pony. All you got to do is hop on and smack that ass."

The only thing that kept their jaw's from dropping off, and their faces from turning red, black, and bluer than they were, was when Tamara overheard them from the next room. She busted in and said, "You Fools! Those are your cousins!" Then, she proceeded to scold them for their shameful behavior. But due to their inebriated condition, they felt no shame– they just giggled and laughed at her to the point of pissing her off. And as such, her lecture fell on deaf ears; she bored them into sleeping off their state of drunken foolishness. Then she made D.A. and Pop promise to say nothing about the incident to anyone.

Samantha's Surprise

Anyway, the following morning marked a turning point for Samantha because she finally got a long-awaited phone call from her Grandmother. The call put her spirits back on track because after she heard her Grandma's voice over the phone, she turned into the sweet, loving, temperamental, spoiled brat that had been waiting to come out.

She was the youngest of the cousins in the family, and for a long time, she had felt awkward being around them; however, now it was easier for her to adapt to her situation. Furthermore, she stuck to Aunt Ella like glue, and she didn't hesitate to tell any of the boys just what she thought of them. She had gained a sense of power that was indirectly backed by Aunt Ella, Uncle Riley, and Rah-Mel.

On the flip side, D.A. was having a fantastic time adapting to this new environment. He took to it as a fish takes to water. His personality blended in with all the other boys in the house. However, their subtle pranks, horseplay, and ridiculous antics were emerging to the point of pissing off their female cousins, and in no time flat, they found out that all of them had a Ph.D. in Bullshit management.

Well, on another note, several weeks had passed since Earlene's bicycle was destroyed by the house nemesis, A.J. But Uncle Alvin was true to his word; he kept his promise by buying her a brand-new ten-speed that afternoon. When he called her to come out back to see it, her face lit up with excitement. She ran up to him, stopped, looked at the bike, and asked him if it was for her. Without saying a word, he handed her a key-chain lock and said, only if you promise to keep it locked up when you're not using it. She said I promise, I promise, Uncle Alvin, and thank you so much. She wrapped her arms around him and gave him a big hug, then she jumped on the bike and took it for a spin around the block.

While she was riding, she was as happy as she could be. Her Uncle Alvin had kept his word, and she was ever so grateful. However, she was also mindful of what had happened to her other bicycle. So, she thought to herself that there was no way in hell that (that rat-ass A.J. was going to steal this bike).

In the meantime, from the kitchen window, A.J. witnessed his dad giving Earlene that new bicycle, and it filled him with envy and contempt. He turned to Chunk, who was watching too, and said, "Ain't this about a bitch! That nappy head heifer got a new bike from my dad, and all I got to ride is that raggedy-ass piece of shit that I've had for the last five years." A.J. was pissed, and Chunk knew the flavor of the Kool-Aid in the back of his mind, and he also knew A.J. was going to get him caught up in some shit with that girl.

Well, anyway, the only one Earlene would trust with her bike was Angie. They took turns riding here and there throughout the day. To the store, the hair shop, the playground, and the park; was

151

the basic limit of their destinations. And at every turn, A.J. was there to beg them to let him ride it —just around the corner, or to the store and right back, so he'd say. And every time he asked, their flat-out answer was "Hell to the Goddamn No!

CHAPTER FIFTEEN

THE AVENGERS

The last week of their stay at Aunt Ella's house was nearly here. The time they had been there seemed to have flown by overnight. Unfortunately, their random acts of rambunctious behavior hadn't changed very much. Nevertheless, with the knowledge and wisdom forthcoming from the enlightened perspective that Aunt Ella had to offer, some, if not all of these kids were bound to see things in a new light.

Furthermore, this strong Black Woman had been falling into bad health for some time now, but regardless, she held on to what she had set out to do. She had a determined spirit, and it was going to play a big part in these kids' reassessment of themselves and their future lifestyles. But, until that time, the gravity of the situation that had been underway remained the same.

THE AVENGERS

It was August 8th, on a Monday morning, when Kim and Samantha put their plan into action. Nearly a week had passed, but they hadn't forgotten about the tumble down the basement steps. They had absolute proof that Popsicle was the one responsible for the act.

They kept their ears open and their mouths shut about the incident and overheard conversations of him and D.A. talking about what he did, and it pissed her off when she saw the shit-eating smirk on their faces when they talked about it.

Nonetheless, today was the day for payback, and all they needed to accomplish their upcoming offensive was the element of surprise. Furthermore, the timing and a good sense of what to expect from that rotten Rat after they did what they planned to do was paramount.

Later that afternoon, they started their plot with a game of 'follow the dollar.' They knew that that money snatching, ice-ball-loving Popsicle would be going through the back hallway past the basement pretty soon because he always went that way to stay out of Aunt Ella's sight to avoid a confrontation with her.

And as such, they were soon going to see if the ten-fresh one-dollar bills they had saved for bait; a bottle of dishwashing liquid, a stiff frying pan, and one of the most gruesome, grotesque zombie mask they could find would do the job they planned to do.

Well, the plan started from the bottom to the top with Samantha in the process of laying dollar bills on every other basement step all the way to the top. Kim stayed in the basement with the zombie mask, waiting for just the right time to put it on and lay down inside Grandma's double-wide deep freezer.

Anyway, when Sam reached the top of the stairs, she stuck a bill halfway underneath the partially opened basement door. Thus, the trap was set.

From past experience, they knew that it would be a cold day in hell before that money snatching runt could resist this temptation, and as such, he fell right into their trap like he was a piece in a jigsaw puzzle. Samantha was sitting at the kitchen table, armed with a bottle of dish soap, when she heard the basement door creep open.

Well, it went just like they predicted. When Popsicle saw the dollar bill sticking from underneath the basement door, his eyes lit up with joy. And when he opened the basement door and saw the other dollar bills on the steps, his eyes sparkled like diamonds, so he proceeded down the steps to pick up every one of them.

So, when he reached the bottom step, he picked up the last dollar and stuck it in his pocket, and, from that point on, Popsicle felt pretty good. He had just made ten dollars and didn't have to run away from anybody to keep it. So, as good as he felt, he looked over at the deep freezer and said to himself, 'why not,' a cherry ice-ball would taste good with this free money. So, he walked over to the deep freezer and opened it up. And right after he did, he screamed like a sissy and pissed in his pants because Kim sat up inside that deep freezer with that zombie mask on and spoke to him like she was the living dead. She said: "Do You Feel Lucky Punk! Huh? Do You?"

Well, as soon as Samantha heard the scream, her job was to

155

open the basement door and squirt the dish soap on all the steps. Well, she managed to get the top half of the steps squirted down, but, as fast as Popsicle was running, half of the steps was all she could manage to do. But, as soon as he reached the top half of the steps, Popsicle lost his footing and slipped on that liquid soap and slid down to the bottom.

Likewise, following the backslide, Popsicle got the ass-whooping of a lifetime. Kim was waiting there with that frying pan, and she beat the living shit out of him with it, and every time he broke loose and ran up the steps to get away, he would slide back down to the bottom, and she'd beat him with wild, whirlwind swings with that frying pan.

Well, soon afterward, D.A. showed up. He was looking for Popsicle, and when he came closer to the basement door, he heard the merciless screams. Then he saw Samantha standing by the half-opened door, giggling and smiling and shouting instructions down the steps at Kim: "That's right, Kim. Beat the meat off that Rat! I bet he won't mess with you again."

By this time, Kim had taken off the mask so he could see who it was going upside his head with that frying pan, and at the same time, she told him: "I know it was you who pushed me down these steps last week, you little Fuckhead! And give me back my money!"

Nevertheless, after a few seconds of seeing his partner being beat into submission, D.A. mustered up just enough nerve to enter that chamber of horror. Samantha tried her best to keep him out, but he struggled with her over the rights to the door and won.

He immediately rushed to get down the steps to rescue him, but little did he know that the top half was covered with dish soap.

When he reached the third step, he lost his footing and went on a bumpy roller coaster ride—he bounced down to the bottom of those steps right beside Popsicle.

Well, feeling helpless and terrified, he soon realized that he was about to receive an ass-whooping right alongside Popsicle. But he managed to get to his feet and run back up the steps to the door. However, when he tried to open it to get out, Samantha banged him in the head with the door and caused him to slip and slide right back down to the bottom.

She had the time of her life because every time she heard him make it to the top of those steps, she banged him in the head with that door and made him slide back down to the bottom, and every time she did, she screamed and hollered laughing.

But, after what seemed like hours of insurmountable pleasure for Samantha, D.A. finally broke through her defense. He managed to get a hand and an arm through the door until he could open it up and pull himself through. But, by the time he had gotten to his feet, Samantha had scrambled.

She took off like a rocket-ship headed for the moon, and by the time D.A. saw the tail end of that rocket-ship, it was flying through the kitchen and out the backdoor. And with fury in his heart, he ran through the kitchen and out the backdoor only to see Samantha standing in the middle of the backyard, right next to Rah-Mel's cage.

Well, D.A. thought his chase was over. Although he was about ten yards away from grabbing her by the throat and shaking the shit out of her, she opened the gate to Rah-Mel's cage and stood behind it.

Rah-Mel sprang out of his cage and growled at D.A., showing him his long, pretty white teeth.

D.A. immediately put on his breaks and came to a Flintstone stop, but he still slid about three feet in front of the ravenous K-9. And, when he did stop, he immediately reversed his charge and started running in the opposite direction, and that's when Samantha shouted: "Get him Rah-Mel!"

Rah-Mel got a hold of one of D.A's raggedy gym shoes and stripped it off his foot. Then, halfway up the back-porch steps, he got hold of a pant leg and ripped it to pieces. Then, with his draws showing, Rah-Mel had his mouth wide open and was about to take a bite out of his ass when Tamara rushed out the back door and stuck the wood-handle of a mop in Rah-Mel's mouth. But Rah-Mel bit through it like it was a tooth-pick, so she turned it around and beat him off with the top end, and that gave D.A. just enough time to crawl to the door and get inside the house.

Anyway, by the time these fallen soldiers saw each other again, D.A. was stretched out on the kitchen floor next to the back door. Popsicle had finally made it up the basement steps and had crawled into the hallway next to the kitchen, and all they could do was look at each other with the agony of defeat written on their faces.

CHAPTER SIXTEEN

OPERATION DOOR JAM

After Kim and Samantha served Popsicle and D.A. a sweet piece of vengeance that morning, later that afternoon, the mischief at the Walker house was on the rise again. The joke that A.J. planned to play on his father was in its developmental stage, but it was coming into focus.

It just so happened that Alvin was waiting for a particular part to reach the auto-parts store. His Cadillac had been down for a whole week, and he was anxious to get it running again. Therefore, he was waiting for a phone call from the parts store, telling him that his part had arrived.

As it turned out, A.J. found out the gist of this information and used it to plot his mischief. So, still being spiteful about his dad getting Earlene a new bicycle, A.J. and Chunk paired up in a quest to piss him off.

Anyway, Rah-Mel's taste of freedom earlier that day must have filled him with the desire to be free from his cage again, because somehow he escaped from his cage and got through the fence in the backyard. Samantha didn't secure the lock on his cage properly when she put him back inside it. However, he still must have found an opening in the gated fence around the backyard.

Nevertheless, he was spotted running down the alley and through the neighborhood. Therefore, Uncle Riley and Alvin had a time-consuming task ahead of them, hunting him down and bringing him back home.

That was undoubtedly the time when A.J. and Chunk conspired to implement "Operation Door Jam." And as such, the first thing they set out to do was find two long pieces of rope. After they found it, they opened the doors to Uncle Riley's station wagon and ran long pieces of the rope underneath the seats– from the passenger side to the driver's side and tied them to the front door handles.

After that, they did the same thing to the back door handles. Then they rolled up all the windows and crawled out the back gate of the station wagon.

Well, soon after that, Alvin and Riley caught Rah-Mel and put him back in his cage, and that's when A.J. and Chunk went through with phase two of their plan. So, from across the alley to the backyard, A.J. used a wireless phone to call the house. Alvin heard the phone ringing and ran into the house to answer it. Then Chunk got on the phone and disguised his voice to make Alvin think he was a salesman; he told him that he could come and pick up his part at the store.

And just like that, they watched Alvin rush out the back door and say, "Come on daddy my part just came in, let's go pick it up at." Well, from that point on, it looked like a scene from the Three

Stooges. And the audience was those two scamps watching from across the alley– laughing their rotten asses off.

Uncle Riley was the first to open his door, and when he did, it opened up about six inches and slammed shut. Likewise, Alvin was doing the same thing at the same time, opening his door and having it pulled shut. At that moment, both of them were confused as hell. They didn't know what was happening, so they tried it again, and again and every time they tried to open their door, the other's door slammed shut. Then they tried the back doors, and again, the same thing happened.

It took a while, but after a few minutes of them looking like two dumb asses, Uncle Riley smelled some foul shit going on.

When they finally figured out what was happening, they heard laughing coming from behind the bushes across the alley. And then they knew that this kind of shit had A.J. and Chunk's name written all over it. When they took a closer look at the car, they saw the ropes attached to the door handles coming from underneath the seat. Uncle Riley looked at Alvin and said: "Well I Will Be Goddamn! Those rotten Mutha-fuckas."

Anyway, to make a long story short, Uncle Riley was so pissed off that he let Rah-Mel back out of his cage. He took him to the back gate and let him run free, all-the-while hoping that Rah-Mel would hunt them down and tare them a new asshole.

Well, after a few minutes, Rah-Mel spotted them, and they spotted Rah-Mel running towards them. So, they took off like two runaway slaves. But, after a short chase down the alley and across the railroad tracks, he caught up with them; they were halfway up a tree holding on to the branches, and Rah-Mel was at the bottom barking– ready to rip them from limb to limb.

So, to teach them a lesson about fucking with him, Grandpa Riley let Rah-Mel babysit them for a while. Uncle Riley let them stay stuck in that tree half the night. However, when Aunt Ella found out what happened and where they were, she furious with Riley, and she nearly had to beg him to get Rah-Mel so the boys could come home.

Well, it took a while for her to break through Riley's stubbornness, but he eventually gave in. But, before he left the house, he stopped by the icebox to get Rah-Mel a treat to reward him for his obedience. When he got to the tree, he patted Rah-Mel on his head and said, "Good Boy."

Then he looked up and saw A.J. and Chunk.. holding on to the branches in the tree for dear life. Then he pulled a long strip of raw steak from his overall's pocket, held it up, and said: "Do you boys see this. This is your ass." Then he tossed the steak to Rah-Mel, and he devoured it in a few seconds. Then Uncle Riley looked up at the boys and said: "Did you see that. That's your ass if you ever fuck with me again. Now, get out of that Goddamn tree and come on home!"

CHAPTER SEVENTEEN

HIP-HOP FEVER

Later that night, the Salt & Pepper girls, Danielle and Sparkle, went on a cross-town adventure. Tamara noticed they were AWOL at12:00 that night. Instead of hearing the usual snoring from their bedroom, there was complete silence. She went to their room and pulled back the covers on their beds and saw piles of clothes, which let her know that those two heifers flew the coop.

Nevertheless, Tamara was fortunate to find a news flyer on the floor next to their beds. It was a useful clue to solve the mystery of their disappearance. It read: "All Night Skate Party 12:00—6:00 A.M. Golden Skates 1209 E. Kemper Rd Ages allowed–18-25— admission $2.00 at door. Contest prizes for best single, couple, and group skating competition. $300.00 for first prize winners, $200.00 for 2nd place, and $100.00 for 3rd."

Well, that was enough to solve the mystery as to where the two hip-hop entertainers were. They were obviously on the other side of town at the skating rink showing off their talent. Tamara knew it all now, but it didn't change the fact that neither one of them was 18. So as reluctant as she was to tell someone, she knew she had to. And that someone was Alvin.

Tamara told him what was going on at 12:30 that night, and the only people rolling around at that time, other than Daniel and Sparkle, was Alvin when he rolled over in his bed and told Tamara, "Fuck Em!" But Tamara persisted in the matter. She screamed, yelled, and ridiculed him with the biggest guilt complex she could muster to get him out of that bed.

Anyway, during their ride to the rink, they both wondered why they would let two under-aged girls in without proper identification, but when they got inside the rink and saw them do their skate routine, they understood why. They looked like two Hollywood moguls.

They had on blonde wigs with a streak of purple dye in them; they were wearing designer sunglasses; black spandex leotards, and they had on red high-top roller skates.

Well, the only way Tamara could identify them was when she spotted the bright red freckles on Danielle's face and Sparkle's big, corn cob calves. They out on the floor shaking their groove-thang—swirling and twirling around in their skates.

All that Alvin and Tamara could do was stand there and watch the show. All of the skaters were good, and, with ten skating couples on the floor, the judges had a hard time declaring a first-place winner. These skaters were zig-zagging around that rink like professionals, doing all sorts of stunts—back-flips, cartwheels, splits, and 360 degree spins. They were skating forward, backward, sideways–sliding through the legs and riding on the backs and shoulders of their partners.

But, those two fifteen-year-old girls held their own. No-one in the family knew they had so much talent. They could do almost anything the other skaters could do, and as such, it turned out that they didn't win the $300 first-place prize, but they did win the $200-second place prize and a trophy. However, the contempt that followed was disheartening.

A couple of the girls knew Danielle and Sparkle, and they knew that neither one of them was 18. Therefore, they objected and contested the win because they were illegitimate prize winners because of their ages. When that news got out, there was a bit of an uproar among the sour-grape losers, but it quickly simmered down. Despite the judges being notified of their ages, there were no other candidates in the competition that even came close to matching the points that Danielle and Sparkle had accumulated, so, the judges sustained their decision.

There was no doubt that the judges would have felt like hypocrites if they took back a second-place prize from the girls after their fair and square performance. They had shown more talent than some of the older girls; however, there was still a group of girls who just wouldn't let it go. Thus, a can of worms was opened that turned into a real live showdown.

Well, the girls may have won two hundred dollars and a trophy for second place in the competition, but it didn't elude from the fact that they did something that was totally irresponsible; they left the house without letting anybody know their whereabouts. And although Alvin was proud of Danielle, he was also upset with her because of what she and Sparkle had done. So, when they approached them, the fleeting look on his face let her know that she was going to face some sort of punishment.

Anyway, Alvin and Tamara had a seat while the girls returned their skates to the check-out counter. And, there was a long line when they got there. Three Amazon warriors were there waiting when they got there: the "Arnold Sisters." One of them approached Sparkle and said: "I know you. You're from Lincoln Heights," Sparkle said: "Yeah, so what." "Girl, you know you ain't hardly no eighteen," she said. Sparkle said: "don't worry about it, we still won second place." And that's when Danielle started to mouth off. "Yeah, at least we won second place. What place did you Hos come in tonight?"

Well, that was just the right thing to say to piss those big, Amazon heifers off because Danielle got hit in the mouth so hard that she back peddled halfway through the rink– back to where her daddy and Tamara were sitting. When Sparkle saw that Danielle was out of commission, she got scared and went wild swinging her skates back and forth at anyone she could hit. And to her surprise, she hit the oldest sister upside her head with one of them. That's when the youngest and the meanest sister of the bunch grabbed Sparkle from behind and held her while her older sister beat on her like she was a punching bag.

Well, Alvin was enraged when he saw his baby girl's face. Blood was trickling from the side of her mouth, and she had a glassy-eyed look on her face.

Nevertheless, the girl that hit her was still on the warpath and headed straight towards them. So, Alvin suddenly jumped to his feet and attacked her big ass. Despite her wolfing, saying: I ain't no ho, little girl, and you better watch your mouth before I …."

Bam! Alvin fired out and ran toward that girl like he was hunting heads. He ran towards her, stuck his right arm out, and closed-lined her across the neck, and she fell flat on her back. When she looked up, she was still lying on the floor, wondering what the hell hit her.

After that windfall, they grabbed hold of Danielle and rushed her to the car. But, on the way out the door, they saw Sparkle being double-teamed by the other two sisters, and Tamara told Alvin to go on— take Danielle to the car; she was going to handle this. But, first things first, she said a short prayer. She said: "Lord, forgive my trespasses as I forgive those who trespass against me. And please, don't let me kill these two bitches."

Tamara walked up behind the oldest sister and tapped her on the shoulder. She said: "Stop beating on my cousin." But the girl just turned and looked down her nose at Tamara and ignored her. Then she turned around and wound up to give Sparkle another gut punch.

In the midst of her doing so, Tamara tapped her shoulder again, but this time the girl made a sudden mojo move. She turned and swung on Tamara and missed. Tamara ducked the punch, and as quick as a cat, she hit that girl in the face with a left-right combination so fast that it stunned her.

So, after the girl recovered and got her bearings together, she tried to charge Tamara like an out of control maniac. Still, Tamara quickly side-stepped her and hit her upside her head with a hard right hook that made her hit her head against a marble counter as she was falling to the floor; she went straight to lullaby land. Then she gave the other sister a grim look and went after her. But after seeing what she did to her oldest sister, she wisely let Sparkle go. She shook her head, threw her hands in the air, and said: "Fuck This Shit!"

Well, it was a long and painful ride home. Their sore bodies would need nursing for the next 48 hours, at least. And during that time, the prevailing thought on their minds was that they paid a hell of a price for two hundred dollars and a second-place trophy.

CHAPTER EIGHTEEN

LAVADA'S LAMENTATION

As they rode back across-town, the sun was coming up. The night of Hip-Hop- fever was over; however, a morning of unsettling drama was ahead. Earlene had been on her usual route to the bathroom several times before Tamara, and the other girls came home. But every time she tried to use the third-floor bathroom, someone was always in it.

So, she had to resort to using the bathroom downstairs on the first floor. Well, this seemed odd to her because someone was still using it when she returned to use it again later that morning.

Anyway, this time, she walked closer to the door to knock on it and heard the sound of someone moaning like they were in pain. So, she knocked on the door to find out who it was, but the only response she heard was, "Go Away! Leave me alone!" And as of that moment, Earlene knew who it was and that something was wrong.

It was apparent from the sound of her moaning and groaning that something was seriously wrong. So, the first person she told was Tamara, who was just about to get in bed. And despite the roller-rink-rumble that she had just been through, she reluctantly obliged her sister's request and went to see what was going on.

It was logical reasoning that pointed out that it had to be Lavada locked in the bathroom because all the other girls were present and accounted for in the bed or somewhere around the house. When Tamara got to the bathroom, she asked if she was alright and if she could do anything to help her, but again, rather than divulging the truth, she shouted for them to go away.

Tamara sensed the stress in her voice and knew that something was seriously wrong. She turned to Earlene and whispered: "go get Lee," while she stayed by the door talking to her and reassuring her that whatever she was going through, everything would be alright.

In a matter of minutes, Earlene returned with Lee. He was in a state of panic after hearing that something was wrong with his baby sister; thus, he tried to coax Lavada out of the bathroom.

He made a little progress by calming her down to the point where she attempted to get up to unlock the bathroom door. However, as she got up from the toilet, they heard her fall. She had lost so much blood that it weakened her, and immediately after hearing her fall, Lee broke open the door and rushed inside.

It was worse than they could imagine—blood was all over the place—on the toilet seat, on the floor, and still oozing from her private area. Lee sat her up and held her in his arms; Earlene ran to get some towels from the linen closet down the hall, and Tamara walked over to the toilet and looked inside–barely able to stomach the sight.

The sight of it gagged her. She immediately covered her mouth with her hand to keep from throwing up. Still, at the same time, after recognizing that there was a partially developed fetus sitting in a pool of blood in the toilet, she threw up anyway and flushed the toilet.

Well, Tamara's heart went out to Lavada. She stood there with a bewildered look on her face, thinking to herself that this little girl must have been going through Hell.

She had been up all night long-suffering on her own because she didn't trust anybody enough to confide in them about her problem. No-one had a clue as to what was going on with her. Anyway, Tamara kept silent about the true nature of Lavada's problem. The only person who needed to know the truth about this situation at that time was Grandma.

Nevertheless, when Earlene returned with the towels and washcloths from the linen closet, she noticed the troubled, hundred-yard stare in Tamara's eyes. From the look on her face, she drew her suspicion about what had happened. She asked Tamara if she was alright, but there was no response, just a long gazing stare, and complete silence.

Nevertheless, when she did respond, she acknowledged her by abruptly saying: "We need an ambulance quick! I'm going to talk to Grandma."

Tamara kept Lavada's miscarriage to herself. She was going to tell her Grandmother, but she was afraid that if Lee found out what had happened, there's no telling how he would react. And if Earlene knew the truth right now, she would run the risk of her telling everybody in the house, so she wisely kept it between herself and her Grandmother.

Anyway, soon after Tamara confided in her, Mrs. Walker immediately called the 911 emergency operator. Fifteen minutes later, she was riding in the back of the ambulance with Lavada on the way to the hospital.

Over the next few days, no-one was the wiser or closer to the truth about Lavada's problem. They all went to visit her in the hospital. But the story was kept plain and simple—she was having severe cramps because of complications with her menstrual cycle.

This tale set well for everyone but her brother Lee; he knew it was much more to it than that, but seeing how his Aunt Ella and Tamara were doing so much to cover up the real details, he decided to go along with them—for now.

So, as it turned out, Lavada finally confided in Aunt Ella and Tamara about the secret that she had been afraid to tell anyone. During those next few days, she explained to them that her stepfather had been sexually abusing her. He threatened to harm her mother if she told her brother, and that he threatened to harm her brother if she told her mother.

Either way, this young thirteen-year-old girl was scared to death, and she saw no other course of action but to do what her stepfather told her to do. Therefore, after Aunt Ella heard her story, she was outraged, but she knew just what to do.,

There was no doubt that if Lee had found out what their stepfather had been doing to his sister, he would have tried to kill him, and he would've wound up in jail for the better part of his life. Instead of letting that happen, Aunt Ella used her wisdom and influence to save Lee from himself and to put that bastard behind bars. She called her friend, who was a councilwoman at city hall. And, after they discussed the issues of her complaint, a warrant for their stepfather's arrest was issued, and on that very same day, they locked that bastard up on statutory rape charges.

CHAPTER NINETEEN

THE ROPE A DOPE

It was Friday, August 12th, and Leon and Leroy were in a funky mood. They wanted to do something– anything to get out of their rut. Leon's stash was gone, and his signs of weed withdrawal were showing. The exuberant sound of his laughter throughout the day was now a spiritless solace of silence.

However, a more practical problem was nagging Leroy. He was worried about replacing the money he spent out of his drug sales. He needed to make a quick hustle to make up the money that wasn't his to spend. He was mad at his self and disgusted with his surroundings because being in that part of the town affected his regular cash flow source, and the exasperation of it all peaked. It showed in his fidgety actions and reactions he had toward everyone that came around him.

Therefore, with the situation being what it was, later that morning, they broke camp and went on a mission to regain their level of comfort.

Leroy's desperate attitude led him to the thought of just using his pistol to corner one of the local dope boys in the neighborhood and robbing him. But, surprisingly, Leon had the clarity to talk him out of that idea because it would only lead to a lifetime of repercussions. Case in point, his Grandfather being on the run all the time because someone was always hot on his ass.

So, they both decided that if they were going to do anything illegal, it would be a quick Sting operation, in which they would be above suspicion and couldn't be held accountable for anything that went down.

Anyway, the area where they planned to pull off their well-devised caper was about a half-mile from Aunt Ella's house. They were in the same rundown neighborhood, but further down the street.

It was a more populated area where there they had a zoning ordinance. There was the business district on one side of the street, with a liquor store, a pawn shop, a grocery store, and some old-rundown apartment buildings sitting in the back of an alley.

On the other side, there was the school district where there was a high school for performing arts and a baseball field that stretched to the end of the block. And as such, the activity in that area included summer school kids going back and forth from one side of the street to the other, and a constant flow of bicycle cops from an inner-city precinct frequently patrolled the area.

Leroy and Leon had a dangerous mission in mind. Nevertheless, they combined their street-savvy, took note of, observed the activities and elements in the surrounding environment, and put all the pieces together in a plausible plan. They came up with one idea after another at first, and nothing seemed to work. But finally, they came up with a plan that they could both agree on and that they were 99% sure would work.

But it was going to take the help of one more player, and that player was Lee, whom they were pretty sure they could talk into helping them. However, that help would come at a nominal price; a ten-piece bucket of fried chicken and a six-pack of Pepsi.

Nevertheless, their next order of business was talking to some of the scumbags in the area to see who could lead them to the drugs. Being new faces in that part of town also meant that there would be trust issues, so keeping a low profile was utmost and necessary to keep from scaring away any prospective connections.

Well, it took some time, but they eventually stumbled onto an O.G. who was a skeptic at first, but he was reluctantly willing to accommodate their needs.

Earlier, they had put the word out on the streets that they were looking for a half-pound of "That Girl" and a pound of some gangster "Bud." In reality, all they had enough money for was an Eight-Ball and a Quarter-pound of Bud. Anyway, that exchange of information was enough to lead them to the only person that could supply that kind of demand. He was a tall, black dread-lock from Jamaica who lived in the West-End– Jamaican Joe.

As it turned out, Leroy knew him because he used to hang out in his neighborhood at times, but he didn't know Leroy in the least. However, true to the game, Leroy still mustered up enough nerve to approach the scary-looking dread to make a bid for some product.

He had just sat down inside a black Ford Escalade at the

corner of the busy intersection. So, he walked to the passenger side window, tapped on it, and signaled for him to roll it down.

Leroy said: "Hey O.G., I need to holler at you, man." he said: "Get inside." Leroy got in the car and immediately told him: "I need an eight-ball and a quarter pound of bud." Jamaican Joe said: "What makes you think I can get those things for you, little nigga? I don't know you!" Leroy said: "Ah, come on, O.G. I know you roll in the best circles, and I know you know some of my people from out the way.

"I know you know one-eye Johnny and Bobby Williams O.G.," And sure enough, when he heard those names, he just chuckled to himself and said: "Yeah I know, Eyeball." Then Leroy mentioned Bobby Williams again and got an even more favorable reaction from him. He asked Leroy: "Is Bobby still fighting those Pitt-bulls?" Leroy said: "Yeah man, Bobby loves those Pitt-bulls, ain't no way he's going to stop fighting them, at least until they're all dead."

Well, fortunately for Leroy, knowing who he knew went a long way. Jamaican Joe turned to look Leroy in his eyes and asked him: "What do you go by." Leroy sat back, looking puzzled by the question, not knowing how to answer. Then he asked him: "Your name, what's your name, little brother?"

But, hesitantly, not wanting to reveal his real name, Leroy quickly made up a name before he answered and told him: "Skycap, they call me Skycap." Joe said: "Skycap! Why is that?" Leroy said: "Because I'm going make so much goddamn money one day, it's going to reach the sky."

Jamaican Joe just chuckled and said: "Look here Sky-crap,

don't waste my fucking time. Do you have money?" Leroy slowly reached in his back pocket and pulled out a thick roll of money with hundred-dollar bills wrapped on the top, and started peeling them back one at a time. He said: "Oh yeah, I got the money O.G." "O.G. looked at the money and said: "That's what I'm talking about– one hour.

Be here in front of this store in one hour, and someone will meet you with your package, Solid." "Solid." "One more thing, don't try to FUCK ME! -----I GOT A GRAVEYARD MIND, A TOMBSTONE DISPOSITION, AND I DON'T MIND DYING!--- I WILL FIND YOU LITTLE NIGGA!

Well, Leroy got out of the car feeling a little bit shaken by what he said, but he also thought that phase one of their plan was in effect, and regardless of what he said, Leroy had already accepted the fact that it was either "get rich or die trying in the streets."

Nonetheless, he got his mind back on the most crucial part of the plan, and that was having Lee ride Earlene's bicycle to the store dressed like a Cincinnati Bicycle cop. From that point on, Leroy could implement a Sting that would wind up in a chase scene. They knew it would take some convincing on Lee's part to get that bicycle from Earlene, but if anybody could do it, he would be the one. They figured that if he told her that he was picking up something for Lavada, she would do it, especially after her recent ordeal.

Nevertheless, although it was almost a sure thing that they could tempt Lee with a bucket of chicken and a six-pack of Pepsi, they still had to stress how important it was for him to wear a blue shirt and Earlene's head-gear. That way, it would resemble the same kind of clothes and head-gear the cops wore. Therefore, they made it a factor contingent upon him getting the bucket of chicken they promised him.

Well, now, it was just a matter of time before they could start the second phase of operation, "Rope-a-Dope."

The proxy that Jamaican Joe sent to deliver the package was AKA ----Raw-Dawg. He was standing in front of the store, inconspicuously looking around to see if he could find someone who fit the description of the contact he was supposed to meet. When Leroy saw Raw-Dawg, he approached him and whispered a few words to him to let him know that he was the mark; after that, he introduced him to Leon. He told him that Leon's would be their lookout man from the street while they took care of their business. With that information known, Leroy and Raw Dawg walked through the long alley's recesses and went inside a condemned building at the other end.

After that, Leroy did his best to stall for enough time for Lee to pedal up on Earlene's bicycle to meet Leon. And while they were inside the building, Leroy took his time inspecting the size, weight, smell, and taste of the product.

Well, they hadn't been inside that abandoned building for more than five minutes, and Leroy had to wonder if he'd have enough time for the final phase of the operation to work.

Nevertheless, the timing was just right, Lee showed up wearing a blue cotton shirt, Bermuda shorts, sneakers, and a safety helmet that made him look just like a bicycle cop, and likewise, Leon played his role as the lookout man. He stopped Lee on the street at the end of the alley and hollered, "5-0 coming, 5-0 coming!"

When Leroy heard him shouting, he cautiously cracked open the door to look. And damned if he didn't nearly go into panic mode himself when he saw Lee sitting on the bike looking identical to a CPD Cop. Furthermore, what also authenticated Lee's presence as a cop was when Lee looked down the alley and shouted to Leroy: "What are you doing down there?"

Hearing Lee's deep voice was enough for Raw Dawg to panic. He gave Leroy a scouring look and shouted: "You set me up Goddammit," then he stuck his package down the front of his pants and jetted out the door.

He was unaware that he was doing precisely what Leroy and Leon thought he would do. When Lee rode down the alley towards the building to meet up with Leroy, he saw him dart out the building running top speed right behind Raw Dawg. Lee had no idea why Leroy was running, but he knew that he wasn't about to let Leroy slip out on that deal for that bucket of fried chicken, so he chased after him while Leroy followed that boy down an alley to a side-street, and watched him haul ass.

Well, even though Leroy was several yards behind, he was still hot on his tail, and he never took his eyes off him. Thus, the realism of being a cop in pursuit of a suspect in this situation that Lee unknowingly caused during his pursuit of Leroy naturally produced a lasting effect of fear in Raw Dawg. And as it turned out, being the three-time-loser that he was, the fear of being caught by the police was on Raw--Dawg's mind.

Anyway, the continuous pursuit from this sequence of actions forced an even more significant reaction. The three-time-loser kept looking back and saw what he thought was a cop right behind

Leroy, and he knew for sure that they would get caught. So, he started unloading everything he had on him—guns, knives, bullets, and for sure, the drug packages he had. He threw everything he had on him in a trash dumpster around the next corner and kept running, determined that he wasn't going back to jail.

By the time Leroy reached the next corner, he had heard the sound of the dumpster lid shut, and he also saw just enough of Raw Dawg's ass running up the street to let him know that they had hit a grand slam.

When Lee caught up with him, he saw Leroy reach inside the dumpster and take something out—he quickly stuck it down in the crotch of his pants. But, before he could figure out what in the hell was going on, Leon caught up with them, and his moment of jubilation started right then and there: "Ehe hee hee hee hee hee hee hee. Ehe hee hee hee hee hee. Ehe hee hee hee hee hee hee."

After that, everything was everything again. Lee got his bucket of chicken and his six-pack of Pepsi. Leon got a stash of weed to keep him happy; they brought a big stuffed teddy-bear and some candy for Lavada, and Leroy was 'Back on the Block.'

CHAPTER TWENTY

THE FREE-STYLE FREE FALL

It was Saturday, August 13th, the day of the Free-Style Amateur Rap Festival. Aspiring rappers and famous performers were here. Washington Park was the spot, and the first prize was a thousand dollars and a recording contract with a major studio.

Ernie and Monty were confident in their ability as rappers, and they were sure this would be a short ladder to stardom. They had been practicing their rap style from the first day they got to their Grandma Ella's house. They were continually rhyming lyrics to different rhythms and beats.

However, they weren't the only aspiring rappers in the house. Earlene and Angie had been practicing their unique style of rap too. So, as it turned out, this event was the opportunity for all of them to compete and compete with a diverse group of talented rappers to earn legitimate recognition as rap artists.

Ernie and Monty signed up under the stage name "The Master Blasters," and Earlene and Angie signed up under "The Elements of Surprise." And despite the hot, early morning heat and humidity, hundreds of people were showing up and piling into the park while the final assembly of the stage was in progress.

.

It was noon, and the show was supposed to start at 1:00 pm. And as the time lingered by, feelings of nervousness took their toll on them. Ernie and Monty were no exception; they knew it was 'shake and bake' time for them. They knew that having a good performance would involve the clear and concise delivery of their rap content and that they needed to be confident with their stage presence.

On the same note, this was Earlene and Angie's first time in front of a large crowd as well; however, they were sure that the content of their rap lyrics and their lewd, lascivious sexual stage performance would win the appeal of the crowd. They were going to do whatever they had to do to win that thousand-dollar first place prize.

Meanwhile, back at Aunt Ella's house, she couldn't know where every member was throughout the day, but she did know the four rap rookies' whereabouts. And although being reluctant about them going to this event—because of the violence that she thought might break out, she gave in to their plea to go after discovering they had already entered the contest.

Furthermore, later that day, she found out her brother, Lester was in town. He and his girlfriend drove down from Detroit this morning to visit her. Also, Erma Jean finally got settled in a new apartment and was coming by to take Tamara and Earlene home with her.

Anyway, back at the festival, do or die time was approaching for Ernie and Monty. Everyone who had gotten onstage so far was booed and heckled. And as the contest continued, new rappers found out what they were made of, and some of them found out that their aspiring rap careers were now a thing of the past.

Nevertheless, Ernie and Monty were the next rappers on deck. They were finally going to get their chance to shine, and as nervous as they were, they still got on that stage and gave it all they had.

Ernie's spit:

I live in the suburbs— go to private schools—I learn my nouns and verbs

And that's all cool. But when I start to talking– thinking it's all good—I sound like a fool in the goddamn Hood! When I get home—Shit ain't much Better—got to live like a saint— aint got a damn bit of cheddar.

Monty's spit: I'm

I live downtown, round a bunch of clowns. I reside in the city–where niggas talk Shit. Expletives and adjectives are all I ever hear— said in strife to describe their way of life— hood-rats and crack heads in the goddamn alley–sucking on a dick just to make a tally.

Together spit:

Uptown downtown, where ever we go—got to get my Shit together—make a cash-money

Roll. Uptown downtown, wherever we go—gonna get our Shit together—make that cash Money flow.

Uptown downtown, where ever we go—got to get my Shit together—make a cash-money Roll.

Uptown downtown, wherever we go—gonna get our Shit together—make that cash Money flow.

Ernie's spit:

Frowns all around me—over here, over there—coming from the honkies—all they do is stare.

Don't want no pity—ain't got no shame—all I want to do is play that cash money game.

Monty's spit:

Rats and roaches running through the halls. Shit on the stairs—piss on the walls.

Open up a book—niggas think you're a fool. Teachers don't care—ain't a damn thing fair—got to use a gas mask just to breathe the fuckin air.

Together spit:

Uptown downtown, where ever we go—got to get my Shit together—make a cash-money Roll.

Uptown downtown, wherever we go—gonna get our Shit together—make that cash Money flow.

Uptown downtown, where ever we go—got to get my Shit together—make a cash-money Roll.

Uptown downtown, wherever we go—gonna get our Shit together—make that cash Money flow.

Ernie and Monty 'rocked the house,' the crowd cheered and gave them a standing ovation. Furthermore, they got a spot in the super showdown to compete with the ten-best semi-finalist.

Earlene and Angie were excited by their performance as well.

They showered them with hugs and kisses when they saw them. The needle on their cockiness meter sprang up to full, and their heads swelled to the size of melons. Their performance inspired Earlene and Angie, and it motivated them to do just as good or better.

Lester and his girlfriend were pulling up through the back alley in a black Cadillac with gold-spoke rims back at the house. He parked across the alley where they got out and made their way through the gate up to the back door. They saw Samantha in the backyard next to Rah-Mel's cage, and Lester spoke to her: "Hey, baby girl, what's your name? She said, "Samantha," and asked: "Who are you?" "I'm Lester, baby doll, and this is Miss Dorthy." At that moment, Rah-Mel grimaced and growled in a low moan, and Samantha quickly told him to hush.

Nonetheless, Lester ignored Rah-Mel's growling because his stomach was growling when his sense of smell picked up on the aroma of collard greens cooking through the screen door. He went to the door, knocked, and hollered inside: "Hey, anybody home." Nobody answered, and he knocked on the door again and said: "Hey, Sis—you in there?"

Well, a part of Aunt Ella's weekend routine was watching Saturday afternoon wrestling. She and all the girls, Tamara, Sparkle, Lavada, and Danielle, were sitting in the front room with their eyes glued to the television. They were watching the wrestling match of the century—Hulk Hogan and Andre the Giant. It was something about watching these big men go at it in the ring and hearing them talk smack that just tickled her to pieces.

Anyway, after his knocks and hollers went unanswered for so long, he decided to come inside and make himself at home. He grabbed a bowl and a fork and dug into that pot of collard greens and cornbread sitting on the stove. And it just so happened that at the same time, Aunt Ella was taking a break from to check on her greens.

When she saw a stranger with his head buried in a bowl, sitting at the table, wolfing down the remaining morsels of her delicious cuisine, she was stirred up. She immediately responded, saying: "Nigga, what in the hell are you doing eating my greens?" Lester just looked up at her with a broad smile, showed her the empty bowl, and said: "What greens?"

She screamed: Lester! You Rascal, I should have known it was you. Boy, how, where did you come from. How long have you been here?" Lester got up and gave her a hug, introduced her to his girlfriend and told her that they just got there this morning. Then he said: "How in the hell have you been, sis? She said: "I've been like I've always been—fine as a can of snuff and just as dusty."

Well, abruptly following that loving moment, Erma Jean showed up. She stepped through the back door and immediately recognized that it was Lester standing next to her mother; she was ecstatic, and she shouted: "Uncle Lester," and ran to greet him with a hug. It had been more than twelve years since the last time he saw his baby niece, and she was a full-grown woman now with all her curves in the right places.

He stood back, took a good look at her, and shouted "Ahhh … … Sollassy" to show his approval for what he saw. However, showing his appreciation for what he saw to that extreme was something that he might have been better off not doing around his girlfriend because it wasn't long before the green-eyed-monster showed up.

Anyway, back at the festival, A.J. showed up with Leroy and Leon. Leroy was on a mission. He wanted to make some fast money, and this was the perfect place to do it. He needed A.J. to lead him to the people he knew who were most likely to cop. So, they rambled through the park from one location to another, making stops along the way to sell and collect money for services rendered.

However, Leroy wasn't the only one on a quest to corner the drug market. They ran across several Jamaican Dreads with the same intention in mind, and they were peddling the same two-toke action ganja that Leroy had auspiciously acquired,

Consequently, it was just a matter of time before the Tot-Lot-Posse showed up. They were in an organized platoon of twenty-five-foot soldiers that were stylishly intimidating when they entered the park.

The militant rebels paraded into the park in a double file of twelve men, with the leader, Black Ice at the helm. They were wearing jeans, sleeveless blue jean jackets, a black armband, and a red, black, and green bandanna wrapped around their forehead. And from the look of things, some serious shit was about to jump off.

Although the park was considered neutral turf, the Posse had always laid claim to its ownership because it was in a part of the city where they lived long before the Dreads even moved to the West End. And it was a well-known fact that the Posse's drug sales were on the decline ever since the Jamaicans move to Cincinnati.

Black Ice was determined to put a stop to it, even if it meant taking out their leader, Jamaican Joe.

Nevertheless, there were a lot of amusing situations occurring in the heart of the festival. The rapping didn't cease to exist on nor off the stage. Earlene had run into a love interest, and Angie was trying to avoid one. A boy was stalking her in the crowd that she didn't know and didn't want to know. There were several occasions when she had to tell him to 'Fuck Off' and leave her alone, but the hard-headed son-of-a-bitch continued to aggravate her.

And whether Earlene knew it or not, she was playing with fire. She had stars in her eyes when a good looking dude at the festival started romancing her. And although he was a lot older than her, and she knew it, it didn't matter to her one bit. Before you know it, she was sitting on his lap swapping slob and listening to his line of bullshit. She was so smitten by his charm that no-one could tell her that he wasn't 'All That and a Bag of Chips.'

Likewise, Monty was awestruck by a fabulous looking girl at the festival. She had teasingly lured him into her presence with her big, beautiful bedroom eyes and her seductive smile; she had his heart pounding like a drum, and his hormones howling like a hound-dog. But his sudden infatuation didn't last long because, while getting his Mack on, he was nearly 'Jacked' when her six-foot-three-inch muscle-bound boyfriend turned around and took her by the hand. They walked away hand in hand, and he gave Monty a glaring stare.

Ernie went through a similar situation when he got his Mack on with one of the finest girls he had ever seen. They were in a deep groove when Peaches showed up to blow his game. When she saw them together, she confronted him with the biggest lie she could tell. That jealous, church crusading hypocrite told him that she was pregnant and that he was the baby's daddy right in front of the girl. Ernie was dumbfounded—he didn't know what to say, and it knocked him right out of the box when it came to having any chance with the girl. Peaches killed that romance before it could even incubate, and he was outraged; he wanted to choke the Shit out of Peaches. Instead, he stood there and said to himself, "What Goes Around is going to Come Around, Bitch!"

Well, at the house, after an hour or so of mingling with the kids and reminiscing, the spiteful eyes of Lester's girlfriend continued to follow and focus on both him and Erma Jean. Nevertheless, Erma Jean went out of her way to be friends with the lady and tried to get to know her and what she liked to do. But her mind was set on thinking the worse and not expecting anything different. Because she knew Lester was a lady's man and a well-seasoned player. Therefore, she insisted on being persistent with her funky, disdainful attitude towards them.

However, Erma Jean played it cool and remained calm and collective about the lady's suspicious nature due to her unusual circumstance. But the snide comments and snobbish remarks that she didn't think Erma Jean heard behind her back were taking a toll on her patience.

Anyway, the fun and laughter continued, and so did her funky behavior. Lester paid absolutely no attention to his girlfriend, and that in itself pissed her off. Thus, the conversations he had were geared toward the members of the family. And the situation came down to his eavesdropping nasty spirited woman overhearing them in a conversation about going to the rap festival in town; that set her on fire.

Immediately following the information she overheard, the car pulling into the driveway sidetracked Lester's attention span–it was Uncle Riley and Alvin. And, the very moment Lester stepped off the porch and walked towards the car, his girlfriend turned to Erma Jean and talked to her like she had a tail between her legs. "I'll be damned if you go anywhere with my man, you Tramp." Erma Jean's fuse was lit. She looked at her with fire in her eyes and said, "Bitch! No The Fuck You Didn't!" A split second later, all that was heard was a loud crack and thump. Before anybody knew what was going on, Erma Jean cold-cocked that woman in her mouth. She fell off the end of the porch and was stretched out flat on her back. But Erma Jean wasn't through with her ass yet.

Meanwhile, before Lester even reached the car, he heard Alvin yelling and pointing behind him. He turned around to look and saw Erma Jean straddled over his woman with a brick in her hands, about to split her wig. Without giving the situation a second thought, he ran over and grabbed his girlfriend by her feet and drug her through Erma Jean's legs just as she was coming down with that brick to scramble her brains.

\

Well, Lester got a taste of the kind of bona-fide-bitch in his baby niece could be that day, and he couldn't rightly blame her for what she did. He knew that sooner or later that his woman's big ass mouth was going to write a check that her little ass couldn't cash. Nevertheless, he picked her up and carried her into the house. When she came to and realized what had happened, she couldn't wait to call a cab and get as far away from that house as fast as she could. And accordingly, Lester's flat out sentiment was Good Godamn Riddance!

It was 3:00 pm, and Washington Park was packed with people shoulder to shoulder. The many vendors from the city were there selling hotdogs, pop, potato chips, and all the usual amenities that a festival provided. Lester and Erma Jean had just made it there. They parked a half-mile away and had to walk the distance due to the lack of parking spaces. And once inside, they had to wiggle and squirm their way through the crowd to find a good enough seat to view the stage. Well, they arrived at just the right time because 'The Elements of Surprise' had just been called to the stage.

And damned if they weren't true to their stage name because what happened next is just what the name implies. Uncle Lester and Erma Jean were sure as hell surprised. So, with no further ado, they got on stage and spat out the lyrics they'd been practicing. Furthermore, they were dressed like two Bengal tigers, wearing orange and black striped spandex bodysuits, boots, and cat-like designer sunglasses.

Earlene's spit:

Hey, little mama's boy, whatcha gonna do? I've been saving this good stuff, especially for you.

You say you wanna Hit It, so come on now and get it.

Ain't got no time to play, so you better come today. Hey, little mama's boy, if you're really hung, come and get this good stuff, come on and get you some. I need me a real man to make my Kitty Cum.

Angie's spit:

Hey, little mama's boy, whatcha gonna do, I got some chocolate pudding here and Umm, it's yummy too. Now, if you can't handle it, or if you're afraid, I'll find me a real man to hit it all day. But if you want some real good Coochie, and if you need a real good Hoochie, then I am the one for you. Come on now, Come On and make my Kitty Cum.

Together spit:

Scratch my Kitty Cat and Lick my Clit—I need me a real man to take away my Itch.

Scratch my Kitty Cat and Suck my Tits—I need me a real man—a man who won't Quit.

Scratch my Kitty Cat and Lick my Clit—I need me a real man to take away my Itch.

Earlene's spit:

Hey little mama's boy, whatcha gonna do, I've been saving this good stuff especially for you.

You say you wanna Hit It, so come on now and get it. I ain't got no time to play, so you better come today. Hey, little mama's boy, if you're really hung, come and get this good stuff, come and get you some. I need me a real man to make my Kitty Cum

Angie's spit:

Hey little mama's boy, whatcha gonna do, I got some chocolate pudding here and Umm it's yummy too. Now, if you can't handle it, or if you're afraid, I'll find me a real man to hit it all day. But if you want some real good Coochie, and if you need a real good

Hoochie, then I am the one for you, come on now. Come on and Make my Kitty Cum.

Scratch my Kitty Cat and Suck my Tits—I need me a real man—a man who won't Quit.

Scratch my Kitty Cat and Lick my Clit—I need me a real man to take away my Itch.

Scratch my Kitty Cat and Suck my Tits—I need me a real man—a man who won't Quit.

Scratch my Kitty Cat and Lick my Clit—I need me a real man to take away my Itch.

Scratch my Kitty Cat and Suck my Tits—I need me a real man—a man who won't Quit.

These girls enticed very male hormone in the vicinity of the stage and then some; however, they didn't get to finish their performance. It took a while, but after Erma Jean recognized the voices on stage, she put two and two together and came up with the correct analysis. She told Uncle Lester: "That's Earlene and Angie on that Goddamn Stage!" And just like a mad black mother, she squirmed her way from the middle of that crowd all the way to the front of that stage and shouted: "Bitch are you Crazy! Get your Ass off that Stage!"

This time the element of surprise was Earlene's mother. Erma Jean ordered both of them off that stage and took matters into her own hands. Earlene was in shock and embarrassed, and it was written all over her and Angie's face. To add to the dismay, the crowd's male members were mad as hell when she pulled them off the stage. They started booing and shouting obscene language. But Erma Jean held steadfast to what she was doing and cussed right back at them. And fortunately, her Uncle Lester was there to watch her back.

Nonetheless, after he saw that Erma Jean safely had the girls into her custody, he recognized some friends and an old flame from the past and somewhat forgot about them for the time being.

Also, unsurprisingly, the one person in the crowd who found pleasure during Earlene and Angie's distressful moment was Peaches. She and her girlfriends were standing right beside the stage when they were abruptly abducted, and they were close enough to exploit the situation with their vindictiveness.

"Peaches shouted: "Who's the Ho now, Ho? Poor little pussycats. Mama's got to take you home and give you a bowl of milk to cool your hot asses off now– don't she."

Well, as hard as it was for them to restrain themselves from retaliating, they did—anyway, for the time being. However, the barrage of insults and name-calling from Peaches and her entourage kept on coming. They were called Ho's, sluts, tramps, and bitches all during Erma Jean's attempt to escort them to her car—and, up until the time that Angie's not-so-secret admirer grabbed her by the ass and disappeared in the crowd.

Well, all hell broke loose after that. Angie was pissed. With all that was happening at the moment, and that kind of Shit was just too much to let slide by without doing something about it. So, she bolted like a wild colt and went on a search and destroy mission to find and confront that bastard.

And at the same time, Earlene bolted in the opposite direction.

selling his weed and his ready-rock to all the well-known pot-heads and crack addicts that A.J. knew. However, it never occurred to them that A.J. was going to introduce them to Raw-Dawg. Raw-Dawg had a booth set up at the rear end of the park selling oils and incents, and when they casually walked up to him, they immediately locked eyes.

But before A.J. could open his mouth to say a word, Raw-Dawg opened up his mouth and said: "I knew I'd see you Motherfuckers again," then he reached for the nine in his belt and pointed it them. However, it was a standoff because Leroy already had his bulldog out, pointing it at Raw-Dawg.

.

Raw Dawg shouted: You got the money you owe me, Motherfucker?" Then Leroy shouted: "I don't owe you jack, Nigga!" A.J. said: "Money? What money? They my cousins, Dawg." Those two Motherfuckers set me up, they the Goddamn Police! Naw, Dawg—you wrong. I swear they my cousins, man." "All I know is that those two Motherfuckers Fucked me out of a quarter pound and a eight-ball. Either they the police or I'm Boo-Boo The Fuckin Fool! Shit if Joe wasn't my brother he would've killed me over that Shit. As a matter of fact, I'm calling Joe right now."

Well, during the millisecond that it took Raw-Dawg to look at the numbers on his phone to dial Jamaican Joe—Leon and Leroy split like a flash of lightning while A.J. stood there watching with the puzzled look of innocence on his face. He just knew that it was All Over for their asses if they caught them, and he knew it was All Over for his ass if he didn't start kissing ass right now like a professional ass kisser.

Meanwhile, Erma Jean was finally catching up to Angie. When Erma Jean saw her, Angie had spotted the ugly son-of-a-bitch who grabbed her ass. He was in a crowd with his other Dread-Lock friends, and a cloud of smoke surrounded them. Well, Erma Jean watched from close by while that petite, fearless little girl walked straight up to that boy and slapped the Shit out of him. His friends were stunned and amused when they saw what happened, but it didn't stop them from laughing at him.

But, seconds after the shock and humiliation wore off, that boy came at her with a backhand and slapped her face so hard that it knocked Angie on her ass. When Erma Jean saw that, she busted a move to that boy and hit him with an overhand right between his eyes and knocked him the fuck out.

She deflated his ass like a busted balloon, and he hit the ground face first. That's when the Dreads stopped laughing—they didn't like seeing that Shit. So, they circled her and Angie and started harassing them and calling them names.

From not too far a distance, Uncle Lester got wind of what was going on and investigated. When he reached them, he couldn't have been timelier. He witnessed that rat son-of-a-bitch draw his fist back to hit Erma Jean in the face. But before any of them knew what was happening, Lester was right behind that asshole. He snatched that boy's arm with one hand, and he had a snub-nose 38 caliber Smith & Wesson in his other hand pressed right upside that boy's head.

He said: "Just Breath Motherfucker! Just breath and be thankful and thoughtful that I haven't blown your goddamn brains out yet and that I still could." He got the message real quick, and so did the rest of his friends. So, Erma Jean and Angie joined up with Lester and started on their way back to get Earlene, Ernie, and Monty. They had had enough drama for one day.

But it wasn't over yet. All of a sudden, they heard the sound of semi-automatic gunfire ripple through the park. Then they heard someone shouting: "They shot Ziggy! They shot Ziggy!" People hit the ground and scurried all about in a panic. People ran into the streets and took cover behind trees, cars, park benches, and whatever they could find to keep from being shot.

The Tot-Lot-Posse was in a war with the West-End Dreads. The Dreads got caught selling drugs on Tot-Lot turf, and fights were breaking out everywhere. Furthermore, Black Ice ordered a hit on Jamaican Joe, whom they thought was in the park at the time. However, they had mistakenly killed his twin brother, Ziggy, who looked, dressed, and wore dreads down to the middle of his back—just like Joe. The security guards were helpless, and the police were out-numbered and out-gunned by gang members on both sides.

After Jamaican Joe got the word that his brother was dead, he went ballistic and declared open season on anybody wearing a red, black, and green bandana. He and his henchmen pulled up in a pickup truck and wreaked havoc on the park's civilian population. They shot and maimed dozens of people just from being suspected of being a member of the Tot-Lot gang.

Leroy and Leon were caught up in the crossfire, trying to reach a haven from this terror driven destruction. Even Uncle Lester hadn't seen this type of warfare since he left Vietnam's jungles in 1969. Nevertheless, he still knew how to be a soldier, and he guided his group of family members to safety. He had them stay low and move quickly behind the trees within the park's perimeter and use any natural obstacle they could find that would protect them from the gunfire.

Anyway, after what seemed like hours of terror and turmoil, dozens of police officers showed up as well as a SWAT team to flush out any snipers that might be in the area. By that time, they had finally reached a safe place to exit from the park, and fortunately, none of them were seriously hurt; however, as they were leaving the park, they turned to take a final look and saw Leroy with his arm draped around Leon's shoulder limping toward them. Somehow Leroy got shot in the ass by a stray bullet.

Anyway, the sight of the dead and maimed, blood-drenched bodies surrounding them was obscene and unbearable to see. The paramedics and rescue teams were everywhere, carting off people by the dozens and rushing them to the hospital, and Leroy was on a stretcher with them.

Anyway, up until this time, no-one had seen or heard from A.J. They knew he was there, but no-one had given him a second thought or taken the time to be concerned about him. That is until they headed across the street and heard a voice say: "Hey Y'all, is it all over now. Is it safe?" They all stopped to look behind them, and then they looked up and saw A, J. high above them perched in a tree scouting the whole area.

So, they asked him: "A.J., what are you doing in that tree?" And A.J. replied: "Shit! Are you kidding? There've been Attempts On My Life!"

CHAPTER TWENTY-ONE

AUNT ELLA'S MESSAGE/THE CONCLUSION

What started as a promising event for aspiring rap artists soon turned into a senseless slaughter. The Free-Style festival turned into a Free Fall for a disaster. At least a dozen ambulances and trauma teams showed up to care for the wounded and to save the lives of near-death victims; over a half dozen news teams there to record this unprecedented event.

Misfortunes in life are brought on by emotions of greed, jealousy, envy, and that all-powerful desire for revenge. And as such, the choices we make under these conditions—good or bad, are how we live. In essence, this is called "Life."

The pranks and antics that went on under Ms. Ella's roof this summer were harmless and innocent, for the most part. However, in a world with so much chaos, confusion, and controversy, under different circumstances, they could lead to more severe consequences—which was the lesson that Mrs. Ella was trying to facilitate.

She knew that good and evil are in all of us, and she referred

She didn't have to go far, though, because her adversary was in plain sight—a few feet away. Therefore, Erma Jean was stuck having to make a split decision—which one to go after. A split second later, she went after Angie because she feared that Angie would be in more danger than Earlene.

Besides, she knew that Ernie and Monty were nearby and could keep an eye on Earlene—and hopefully, they'd make sure she didn't kill anybody. Anyway, Earlene pushed her way through a crowd of people to reach Peaches and her girlfriends; she just walked up to her and slapped her upside her head. And the sting from the slap so powerful that it had Peaches seeing stars. She staggered backward into the arms of her girlfriends, who held her up. But Earlene wasn't through with her yet. She hollered: "What you going to do now, Pretty Bitch!" Well, just then, Peaches got her focus back and ran toward Earlene, swinging her arms—scratching and clawing at Earlene's face.

Ernie and Monty were watching from the sidelines, and they got a kick out of watching Peaches get her ass kicked—especially Ernie, who felt like she deserves to get her ass kicked for blowing his game with that girl earlier, so he wasn't going to do a damn thing to stop it. However, he changed his mind after seeing Earlene sitting on top of Peaches, beating her head back and forth like it was in a pinball machine.

Peaches was damn near unconscious. Earlene was on top of her, batting her head from side to side. And it took Ernie and Monty to pull Earlene off of her.

Well, meanwhile, on the other end of the park, Leon, Leroy, and A.J. were still hanging tough. Leroy was making a killing to these elements as "The Seeds of Temptation." She knew that they grow stronger as we get older and that they could lead to dangerous outcomes without proper guidance. And she also knew that the best way to reroute temptation and the urge for revenge is with the advice that comes from having strong morals and having a healthy value system.

That was the basis of her motive to have them attend church services with her every Sunday. Furthermore, this wise old lady was well aware that most of these kids' lives had been allocated by single-parent households, living with Grandparents or other family members, living in foster homes, or just living in general dysfunctional settings. However, she felt like she had an obligation to help these children learn who they are, where they come from, and about life by teaching them a few profound: Lessons from the Bible.

The Lesson from (Jonah)

Jonah learns a valuable lesson about the Lord's mercy and forgiveness. He learns that it extends to all people who repent and believe in the Lord—even his enemy and he also learns that he should be a shining light to the people that have gone astray."

The Lesson from (Samson & Delilah)

"Although he was a failure, he still accomplished the mission that God-assigned him to do. So, the lesson from this is that Samson is just like you and me when we give ourselves over to sin.

When we are in a state of sin, we can easily be deceived because the truth becomes impossible to see. But no matter how far you've fallen away from God, and no matter how big you've failed, it's never too late to humble yourself and return to God."

Lesson from (The Story Job) of

"The story of "Job" will also teach you a lesson. That lesson is to always keep your faith in God and worship him despite the hardships in your life. Job was a man who had everything you can imagine in his time. He had it all: A large family, wealth, and blessings of every kind imaginable, but he lost it all and still remained faithful to God and received more and more immense blessings from God than he had before.

The Lesson from (The Story Of Abraham)

"The lesson from the story of Abraham is an example of how you should have genuine faith in God. And how our faith should result in us doing good things. The faith that you have inside you should result in an outward change of your behavior. If it's doesn't, then you may not be of genuine faith at all."

The Conclusion

"You are the 5th generation of great-grandsons and grand-daughters of Bedford and Liza Le Grand. Bedford Le Grand was born in 1805 in North Carolina, and he was a slave. Every one of you is a descendant of an African slave, and every one of you is the descendant of an African slave that came from a bloodline of African Kings, Queens, and Warriors."

"Your greatness stems from your bloodline. The blood inside you holds the key to who you are and the proof that you have yet to realize. Until you know who you are, you will never do the great things that you are capable of doing. So walk tall and be proud of who you are, and learn how to love yourself and respect all people to the best of your ability. Until you really know how to love yourself, you will never know how to love anyone else."

"Children, try to lead peaceful, productive lives and always give praise to God. The tricky part of life is that God gave us free will to choose the direction and the way that we want to live our lives; be smart and choose wisely. Let your faith in God grow from this day forward; your faith and your hard work will get you through the hard times when everything else fails."

As things turned out, most of these kids took to heart the message that Mrs. Walker had to tell them. They understood the correlation between Bible stories and the things that were happening in their lives. The recollection of these four lessons added knowledge and wisdom to their everyday lives and profoundly affected them as individuals. Most of them immediately took heed of what she said and started living their lives from a positive perspective.

Unfortunately, a few of them didn't fully comprehend what was said to them and continued on a path of needless mishaps and mayhem, and somehow Aunt Ella knew that would happen too.

Nevertheless, six weeks later, Mrs. Walker passed away. She was in Heaven wearing the wings of an angel. One of the largest funerals in the city was held. Friends and relatives from all over the country were there to show respect to the grieving family. Most assuredly, her great-nieces, nephews, and grandkids were all there.

Tears were flowing, and sadness overwhelmed their hearts. A sea of the grave, gloomy faces filled a small, Holiness church on the hill. The immediate family sat down front at a loss for words bereaving with tears and dismay– crying out loud throughout the funeral.

As the preacher read her obituary aloud; it told a story about her endless accomplishments and contributions as a humanitarian, housewife, and lifelong mother dedicated to her children and family.

A Few Years Later

Although A.J. used to attend church regularly, he was now a skeptic about going to church– especially after his Grandmother's death. He also had doubts about the existence of God. However, one day he was in a tragic car accident and had a near-death experience that caused him to reassess God. And as it turned out, after a spiritual awakening, he resumed his faith in the higher power of God, and he and Walter turned their lives around by focusing on their God-given talents. A.J. got his real estate license and started flipping houses a few years later. He is married now with three kids and is doing very well.

Walter went back to Atlanta, joined the church, and started

working as a salesman for a well-known car dealership. Now, at twenty-five, he is one of the top salesmen in his area and will soon have his car dealership.

Leon and Leroy were birds of a feather that strayed in a different direction. The bullet that found its way to Leroy's behind hadn't taught him much about life, and it wasn't the last time he got shot. Anyway, as soon as they turned eighteen, they both did time in prison. Leon did a year in the pen with three years parole on the shelf. Leroy did a mandatory five years for drug solicitation and possession of an illegal firearm. Nonetheless, they're doing fine now.

When he was in jail, Leon got his GED, went through a 12-step program, and is now working as a drug counselor at a rehab facility. At night he attends the University of Cincinnati and is taking abnormal psychology courses to get his bachelor's degree.

Leroy did an about-face and turned his life over to the Lord. He went to truck driving school and worked as an over-the-road truck driver making enough money to get his mind off the fast cash he made in the streets.

D.A. and Lee both had the physical size and the natural talent to play professional sports. However, Lee turned down several scholarships to play football. Instead, he finished high school and was offered a position as a manager at a fast-food restaurant. And Right now, he is a regional manager over a chain of Wendy's in Southwestern Ohio.

D.A. got a scholarship to play basketball at Eastern Kentucky University. But unfortunately, he played for two years and injured his ACL. He recovered, but he never felt he would be the same player that he had been. He sacrificed his love for a career playing basketball and settled for a degree in corrections and a minor in recreation. He works as a Park Ranger in peak seasons and as a middle school basketball coach during basketball season.

Little Gary—AKA—Popsicle, continued to go on a path of adverse trials and tribulations; he didn't get his act together until sometime later. However, he was fortunate to have gone to jail as soon as he turned eighteen; if not, he more than likely would have wound up dead. Anyway, during his three-year stretch, he eventually opened his eyes and saw the light. He got his high school equivalency, and through his love for money, he used his God-given ability. He gained an interest in accounting, and when he got out, he went through a two-year training course and adapted to a natural affinity for doing tax returns. He now works as a freelance tax return specialist and consultant.

Monty and Ernie continued to follow through with their ability as a rap artist. They started their rap group and had professional careers as "The Master Blasters," performing in concerts all around the United States, but after three years, they broke up. Monty still lives in L.A. and works behind the scenes as a music producer with various rap artists. And Ernie followed his boyhood interest in photography and somehow flipped it into a Hollywood career as a cinematographer.

When it came to the girls, they found the courage to be proud of who they were, the power to change the things they could change, and the wisdom to know the things they couldn't change.

Danielle and Sparkle went after what they wanted to do in the entertainment field. Sparkle wanted to be an actor on stage

DAVE WILLIAMS (MAED)

or in the movies, and Danielle wanted to be a dancer. They both attended a school of performing arts, and they followed up by taking professional classes in choreography and acting. Danielle moved to New York City, where she has performed in several Broadway musicals. Sparkle moved to L.A. where she was discovered by talent scouts that set her up in roles as an actor in several drama scenes at Paramount Studios in Hollywood. Now they're both awaiting offers for a breakout performance on stage or screen.

Lavada made things simple for herself, despite all her hard work getting a degree. She went to college and studied child psychology, and became a child care specialist. She now works with children with disabilities and has a titled social work position for the Department of Job and Family Services.

Earlene and Angie got scholarships to attend Howard University to study Law. They recently passed the Bar Exam and are practicing attorneys. Earlene's specialty is in criminal Law, and she works as a defense attorney in Washington D.C. Angie's specialty is corporate Law, and she works as a special advisor and liaison collaborator on foreign affairs.

Well, after that memorable summertime experience during the mid-1990s, the eldest cousins—Kim and Tamara, decided to go into the business of saving souls. A few years afterward, they enrolled in a divinity college and ultimately received Doctorate Degrees in Theology and later served as pastors in the church. Right now, they aspire to serve as pastors in their churches so they can change the world one soul at a time.

Last but not least is eight-year-old Samantha, who turned out to be the most phenomenal cousin out of the group. At the age of sixteen, she was accepted into Harvard Law School, and she has been consumed with a passion for serving the public in the political arena ever since she has been there.

However, her most profound passion lies in her undying aspiration to become the first African American Woman President of the United States.

CPSIA information can be obtained
at www.ICGtesting.com
Printed in the USA
LVHW031135060221
678565LV00001B/16